Charlotte and the Twelve

A Steele Secrets Story

Andi Cumbo-Floyd

Book Layout & Design ©2013 - BookDesignTemplates.com
Proofreading by Laurie Jensen – lsjensen@embarqmail.com

Ordering Information:
Quantity sales. Special discounts are available on quantity pur-
chases by corporations, associations, and others. For details,
contact the author at the address above.

Charlotte and the Twelve/ Andi Cumbo-Floyd. -- 1st ed.
ISBN 978-1-5403063-0-2

Other Books in the *Steele Secrets* Series:

Steele Secrets

Silence at the Lock

Dedicated to the amazing individuals and communities who are preserving Rosenwald Schools across the South.

I did then what I knew how to do. Now that I know better, I do better.

–Maya Angelou

1.

When my eyes flashed open from a blink, I was no longer staring at the snow falling outside our front door. Instead, I was inside a sagging building with huge windows. The snow was still falling, but now it didn't matter if we had school or not. Now, I had to figure out what adventure the universe, God, a ghost, whoever had taken me on. I never could quite explain what had happened the last time I'd mysteriously appeared somewhere, and so why would I be able to do it now.

Here's what I know:

If it's happened once, it can happen again.

People say that kind of stuff about bad boyfriends and shoplifters, but it's true of the good stuff, too . . . like, say, the way a girl might get transported, teleported, reassembled in a place that she hadn't been a second before.

Ah, but I'm being cryptic. I wonder where that expression came from—cryptic as intentionally vague . . . does it come from "crypt," like a grave? If so, is my experience with graves going to haunt my language forever now?

Also, sorry for the haunting pun. My ghost experiences have shaped me, I guess.

So here I was in a big room—I'm terrible with sizes, but let's say the size of a Tastee Freez dining room—and there were two *huge* windows in front of me. Even on this early January morning, I could see well within the room because of these windows.

I stood still a while to get my bearings AND because I wasn't sure I wouldn't fall through the floor if I took a step. The prime days of this room were long gone, and I could see over in the corner that water had made its way down the walls for a long while now.

Kitty-corner to the water stain, I saw a big jumble of wood and metal that looked kind of like those old desks I've seen in the big houses around here, the ones that are used as decorations in a front hall. I eased my way over, testing every step as I went. It was winter, so I knew I didn't have to worry about snakes if I put my foot through the floor, but I didn't really want to have shards of wood piercing my teddy bear PJ pants.

As I got closer, I found that these were, indeed, desks. Old desks. Dusty for sure, but also filmed with the grime of years and use. I bent low and put my hand against the seat back in front of me to steady myself as I got a closer look.

That's when I saw her.

My last experience with a ghost had been wonderful and not at all scary. But still, having the figure of a young girl in a white dress appear right by your side—that'll take out anyone's breath.

I jumped back and stared. Yep, there she was—a tiny slip of a girl—probably about six, with a halo of brown hair framing a thin face that ended in a softly-pointed chin.

She looked absolutely terrified.

I knelt down a couple of feet in front of her and said, "My name's Mary. What's your name?"

She stared at me with her wide, soft eyes for a minute longer. "Henrietta Lovely Jones." Her voice was almost a whisper. It sounded like a kitten's mew.

"It's nice to meet you, Henrietta Lovely Jones. Do you live around here?" Now, in the past couple of months, I had done some reading about ghosts, and Henrietta Lovely Jones was definitely a ghost. When you can see a person and also see through them, it's a pretty clear sign.

The tiny girl began to cry, and so I moved closer and sat down. "Oh, sweetie, what is it? Sit down here with me and tell me about it."

January in the Virginia mountains is cold, and I was wearing a t-shirt I caught at a UVA basketball game about three years ago and those cotton teddy bear PJs I mentioned. Henrietta was in this white dress with fine lace around the collars and sleeves, and her arms and legs were unclothed; and while I had on sheepskin slippers—a gift from Mom this past Christmas—her feet were bare. Yet, I was shivering like the dickens, and she seemed to give off that perfect gentle heat that children do. I wanted to hold her—as comfort for her and warmth for me.

Henrietta plopped down on the wide, wooden planks beside me and leaned her shoulder against mine. She wasn't actually warm, but the gesture was sweet anyway. I glanced down at the space where my pinkish, white skin met her golden brown elbow and leaned in.

"I live here, I guess," she said. "But I used to live just up the road a ways. I haven't been able to go home for a long, long time." Her face broke open with the sorrow only a child has not yet learned to hide. She wailed long, shuddering sobs that wound around my heart and squeezed.

I wrapped my arm around her and pulled her into my lap. "Oh, Miss Henrietta, I'm so sorry. I'm so sorry. Maybe I can help?"

This quieted her a bit, and she looked up into my face with eyes so wide I thought I'd be able to see the moon behind them.

"Are you here by yourself?" I said quietly.

She shook her head over and over again.

"Okay, who is here with you?" I wasn't scared of ghosts, but the idea of a group of them made my voice a little shaky.

"All us kids is still here. Miss Braxton is here, too."

I looked around, but I didn't see anyone . . . not yet. I set Henrietta on the ground so I could stand, then scooped her against my hip. She weighed little more than a gallon of milk.

I walked over and placed my hands on every desk in that little pile. As I watched, a dozen children— girls in simple calico dresses and boys in cotton pants and shirts with buttons— appeared around me, each of their faces turned toward mine with wonder and fear.

Then, I saw her, a regal woman in a blue-flowered dress. She was at the back of the room, and she didn't look happy to see me.

I smiled because that's what I do when I'm nervous or scared or unsure. I smile . . . not a bright, wide-open at the eyes smile, but that one that's tight in the corners of my mouth, like that emoji with the clenched teeth. I mean to appear harmless, but I fear I may look more like I've just had some pretty awful dental work.

The woman did not smile back.

I studied her face—unlined and smooth, the color of a sparrow's wings, and eyes deep brown and wary, not harsh or threatening—fearful, not protective. I took a step forward, and the children moved toward her, gathering around her hips like chicks under their mother's wings.

"My name is Mary," I said from where I stood.

"That's Miss Braxton," Henrietta whispered up at me. I looked down and realized I was still holding the child against my hip. I let her slip gently to the floor, and she scampered over to Miss Braxton's side.

As the woman bent to look the tiny girl in the face, I studied her. She was thin and quite tall, six feet maybe, and she carried herself with the posture Mom always wished I had. Her dress wasn't fancy, but I could tell it was well cared for because the pleats at her waist were pressed flat. I'd never had a piece of clothing with that fresh a crease, but that may be because I hate to even look at an iron.

Miss Braxton stood and walked toward me. I took a step back and felt the back of my knee connect with the pile of desks. I was going over, but then Miss Braxton's firm hand gripped my arm and pulled me upright. We were standing face to face, well, more like face to shoulder, since I was almost six inches shorter than her.

She stared at me and then said in a firm, clear voice, "Why are you here, Miss?"

Good question, I thought. A few months ago, when I'd mysteriously appeared in that old cemetery, I'd asked Moses—another ghost—that very thing, and it took us months to figure out the answer.

"I'm not really sure, Miss Braxton. Actually, I'm not even sure where I am. Maybe you can help with that."

"You're in the Shady Run Rosenwald School, ma'am. *My* school." I didn't miss the emphasis.

"Oh." I walked over to the big window past Miss Braxton and looked out. Just to the right and off a ways, I saw the familiar outline of a flat ridgeline—House Mountain. Then to the left, I could see the rest of that Blue Ridge peeling away. Yep, I was still in Terra Linda, but I didn't know this place, didn't recognize it at all. "Where in Terra Linda are we, then?"

Miss Braxton studied my face. "You're in Bliss Hollow. Up above the river, ma'am. But I expect you've never been up this way before."

She was right. I had no idea where Bliss Hollow was, but given that this woman and these children were clearly not from 2015, I wasn't sure that I would even call this place by the same name. For all I knew, it would be Taco Truck Road now.

The children had begun to spread out. Two boys had marbles in the corner, each one taking a turn at flicking a marble into another. I wondered if that hurt their fingers—sure looked like it did. A group of girls, including Henrietta, were tucked into a corner, a doll on one child's lap, and in the universal language of young children, I knew they were playing school.

Miss Braxton studied them and then gestured to me, a gentle wave of her hand, and led me to the corner of the room by a door that clearly went into the backyard of this building. "Miss, I don't mean to be rude," she said in a voice solid despite its whisper, "but I'm quite confused by your presence here." She paused and tilted her head to look at me. "You don't seem that puzzled at all, though."

Oh, I was puzzled alright, but not that I was here. I knew that part would sort itself. I was more confused about just where *here* was. "Oh, well, you see, this happens to me sometimes, I just show up places and meet the folks who still live there."

She squinted a bit and waited. It was this waiting that confirmed what I suspected—this woman was a teacher. Only a teacher knows that if you wait long enough someone will give you more information.

I didn't disappoint. "I mean, I know you are all ghosts."

She pulled her head back quickly.

"Oh, don't worry. I'm not scared, and I'm not going to go tell anyone. I just know, is all."

With a gentle tug down on the skirt of her dress, Miss Braxton took a few steps away toward the window behind her. She watched the trees outside as her hand worried the seam of her right sleeve.

It was my turn to wait, so I leaned my shoulder against the wall by the window and studied the floor, while I considered what I knew. Clearly this was a school, a school for black children. These people had been alive a long time back but not so long as Moses in the graveyard because their clothes were more like mine than his had been, although still none of the girls nor Miss Braxton wore pants.

"Yes, miss. Yes, we're ghosts. We've been here sixty years, if I'm counting the autumns right."

I pulled my shoulder from the door and looked into her eyes.

"Why are you here? All of you? Why here in this school?"

"Well, Miss, that's a long story. A long, long story."

She turned back to the window.

2.

I know about long stories, generations-long stories, AND I know that when people say, "It's a long story," even ghost people, they mean either, "Now's not the time," or really, "I'm not interested in sharing it with you." Southerners are nothing if not mannerly through passive aggression.

So when Miss Braxton said that, I nodded. Then, I screeched one of those sturdy, old desks out from the corner and squeezed my rear into it. I wasn't thinking she'd tell me the story if I stayed. I wasn't even really ready to hear the story, I think. Nope, I was just here because the universe or fate or God or whatever had dropped me here, and I knew from experience that this meant something.

I did pause to think about Mom at home, to consider if she would be worried. She would, but then, she'd also wonder if it had happened again, like the last time. So she'd give me a bit before she called Isaiah and came looking. I'd not stay too long, but I also had the question of how I'd get back home. Or even where home was relative to here exactly.

Now, though, I had people to think about—kids—and while I didn't think myself their savior or fancy that I had to do some *Supernatural* style thing where I had to hunt down their bones, pour salt on them, and burn them, I did know that I was there for some reason that mattered because of who I was. As odd as that seemed.

I sat and watched the kids for a while. Eventually, Miss Braxton began moving around, talking to each of them and letting the littlest ones hold onto her legs a moment here and there. She kneeled low and looked them in the eye, and they told her about the birds they had seen with a berry in their beaks and how this one time they'd seen a bunny after it was hit by a car.

I wondered if she still tried to do lessons with them, but then, I didn't really know how this worked. Did the children even know they were dead? And were all of these people really here when someone wasn't here to see them? Did they arrive at the time school started every day and then disappear at the closing bell? Did that bell ring? Was there a bell?

You can see how I could spiral myself into a lot of questions with very little way to answer them unless I stayed put.

Eventually, Miss Braxton looked my way again, and I pulled a desk over for her. She sat down sideways in the opening between the desk and the seat back, resting about one inch of her rear on the seat. If I sat that way, the desk would either tip over or I'd slide right off of it onto the floor. I was nothing if totally ungraceful.

She looked at me out of the corner of her eye and asked again, "Why, Mary," she said my name softly but with a force of iron behind it, "are you here? Every day, the children and I are here, but today is the first day we've ever had a visitor. Rather, you're the first visitor who can see us."

I tilted my head. "Yeah?"

"Sometimes, neighborhood children come in here to drink spirits or do other things of which I will not speak. Every once in a while, a child who went to school here stops by, too, bringing his children or grandchildren with him." She paused and smiled. "I so love seeing their faces and hearing their voices gone all deep with years. Micah comes in regularly, too, just to check on things. But none of them can see the children or me."

I nodded. That seems to be the way of these things.

"So Mary, how come it is that you can see us, hear us, touch us, even when no one else can?"

I could tell by the hesitation before she said "us" that she was not accustomed to thinking of herself and the children as a group. She was their teacher, and she knew a distance had to be kept. All of my teachers had been the same, the kind ones at least. They'd chat and hear my stories, listen if I cried about a grade or something mean someone said. But they didn't share their private stories or pains. Teachers were not the friends of their students, and this seemed right to me. Smart. Useful. Loving, even.

"I'm not right sure, Miss Braxton. I'm not right sure. But I suspect we can figure it out if we get to know each other a bit." I tucked my head. I felt presumptuous asking this polished woman with her perfect posture if we could be friends.

I heard her shift in her seat, and when I peeled my eyes up to her face, she was looking at me. "I suppose that would be just fine, Mary, but only if you call me Charlotte."

I smiled. "Sounds good to me, Charlotte. Absolutely."

Just then, out of the corner of my eye, I saw a flash of white and turned just in time to catch Henrietta as she flew into my lap, her eyes wide. "He's here," she whispered.

I barely had time to put Henrietta down when the door flew open and a large man with ham-hands stomped in. (Yeah, I know, pointing out that someone's hands are like giant hams isn't exactly nice, but seriously, these suckers were the size of entire pork shoulders and not some vegan pig shoulders, either.)

He had on a long trench coat and a wide-brimmed hat, and I thought he looked like a bounty hunter if a bounty hunter was really angry and not just a person with a job to do. His face was twisted with rage, really twisted, like his eye was almost at the corner of his mouth, and his hands were in fists before him as if he could open his fingers and slam us all against the wall at will.

I glanced over at Charlotte and the children. She had gathered them behind her in the corner and was frantically urging me over to them with her eyes. I took a quick step that way but stopped short when he spoke.

"Who are you?" His voice was gravel that had been sharpened, and the pitch of it made me feel like the veins in my neck were rumbling.

Now might be a good time for me to share that I'm not easily scared most of the time. I'm not scared of change or going new places or eating new foods. But I am scared of one thing—disappointing people . . . even big, scary guys who obviously terrify small children and their teacher.

"I'm Mary Steele," I squeaked and took a step forward with my hand outstretched. (I wasn't really much of a hand-shaker, to be honest, more of a hugger if necessary or a friendly-waver, but I was sure shaking a lot of hands today.) I could feel Henrietta leaning the top of her body as far behind me as she could while I moved to this man.

But she needn't have worried because I stopped moving as soon as he spoke again.

"You are trespassing."

Normally, the accusation of a crime would have made me defensive and sheepish, and I would have said, "Yes, sir," and made my way out the door. But two things stopped me: first, he was in front of the door, and I didn't really think my five-feet-five-inch frame could push a man well over six feet and as broad at the shoulders as the doorframe.

Yet, it was the second reason that really stopped me. For just a split second, I saw doubt pass behind his eyes. It was like a flicker, a wiggle in his corner, a flinch at his tear duct. Something, something that told me he wasn't so sure of that statement.

I took a deep breath and said, "That may well be, but I don't see as how I'm doing any harm." I paused and screwed the courage up from my belly button and said, "Can I ask what you're doing here?"

I heard Charlotte draw in a sharp breath.

"I own this school, woman." This time he marched to me and leaned down to look into my eyes. "I own it."

His face was folded the way faces get when they've lived through hard things. His cheeks came forward and down into what people, I think, call jowls, and his brow was sunken as if life had sat heavy on his head for his days. His skin was the color of ash that doesn't get burned all the way up, and his eyes were pools of brown so dark that they could have been black.

I didn't lean back, although that took a profound act of will. Instead, I slid my right arm behind me and grabbed my left elbow. "Oh, I see. You own this building. Well, I am sorry for being on your property without permission. I meant no harm. Was just taking a look around."

He stepped back a bit, and I took this as a sign that we might be—as they said on *Criminal Minds*—deescalating the situation. I glanced over my shoulder to Charlotte.

"What are you looking at?!"

I saw Henrietta jet behind Charlotte's skirt and glanced quickly up to the man's face. He wasn't trailing her at all. He couldn't see her or any of the other ghosts.

I looked quickly down to the ground. "Just taking a look at this interesting building."

I saw his shoulders drop, probably because he thought he was dealing with a wacko who came out at seven-thirty on a January morning in her pajamas. Then he said, "Well, you best be going."

"No problem." I still wasn't sure what I'd do about getting home in the snow in PJs and slippers, but I thought it might be wiser to take my chances there than with this angry man. "Do you mind if I ask one question before I go?"

I saw his shoulders stiffen, but then he gave me a brisk nod.

"When was this school closed?"

"1954. The year I finished eleventh grade." His face softened a smidge at his jaws.

"Oh, so you went to school here?"

"I did." He looked at me, then suddenly turned his head to look into the corner where Charlotte and the children cowered. "Well, until that day. I went here until that day when . . ."

He looked up suddenly as if realizing he was answering more than one question. Now his face looked only tired, "weary," Mom would say. I began moving toward the door.

"Mary, is that what you said your name was?"

I turned back to face him from the doorway. "Yes, sir, Mary Steele. And I really didn't mean any harm. I was just curious about this lovely old building that now sits empty. I live just over that way on Pleasant Mountain Road. I'm sorry to have intruded."

He sighed. "It's okay, Mary. I just thought you were another kid in here trying to make trouble." He took a glance around the room. "No harm done."

"Thank you, um . . ."

"Tindall. Micah Tindall."

"Nice to meet you, Mr. Tindall. Have a good day."

I walked out into the snow. We definitely were not going to have school today, which was good because I was probably going to die of exposure before I got home.

I walked across the ever-whitening grass and out to the gravel road before me. I still wasn't quite sure where I was, so I figured I'd probably have to go down the mountain to get back up mine and headed off, grateful at least that Mom had gotten me slippers with soles for Christmas.

Just then, a car pulled up beside me, and Mr. Tindall opened his window. "Child, you cannot walk in this. Get in. I'll get you home."

Some people might take the chance of hypothermia over a ride from a strange and somewhat angry man. I was not one of those people.

3.

It turned out I was only about a mile from home. A right turn, a left, and then a right onto my road. In the hollows of the mountains, roads run like streams in the crevices, and so I just hadn't been up that one yet.

The ride was mostly quiet. I told Mr. Tindall where to go. He nodded. When we pulled into my driveway, I said, "Thank you," and he said a solemn, "Welcome." I climbed out, and he drove away. Simple.

Well, simple until I got to the front door and saw Mom's face. Her jaw was set so tight she could have split a penny with her molars. She stepped aside and let me into the house, and I headed right for the fireplace and the roaring fire.

I didn't speak. I wasn't stupid. It took her a while to calm down enough to come over and say,

"Mary Steele, what were you thinking? Taking a ride with a stranger? I thought you were wiser than that."

I nodded and looked her in the eye. I kept my hands by the fire. I stayed silent. See, I was wise.

"What happened? Why were you gone? Where did you go?"

I looked at her again and took a deep breath.

She continued, "Are you okay? You look okay, but ARE you okay?"

Now, now was the time to say something, after Mom had gone from anger to curiosity to concern. "I'm fine. Very cold. But totally fine. Really." I wiggled my fingers and did a little rump shake to prove it.

Mom smiled and grabbed a blanket off the back of the couch and draped it over my shoulders. Then, she sat down.

I waddled over with the blue blanket snug around as much as of me as I could handle without tipping over and plopped down next to her. Right next to her. Body heat was a precious commodity at the moment.

Then, I told her the whole story. We'd been through this mysterious disappear-reappear thing before, so we moved right to the why of that place and those ghosts. And Micah Tindall. Who was Micah Tindall?

"He said he was the owner of the building and that he went to school there, but . . ." I began.

"Did you think he was lying?"

"Oh, no, not at all. He was angry and upset with me for sure, but he seemed to be telling the truth. But maybe not all of it. I don't know. Just something about the way he moved in that place, like he was hesitant to shift the air at all . . ." As we'd walked out of the school, I'd seen Mr. Tindall hesitate with each step, his foot a bit off the floor for a second before he pushed himself further.

"So maybe he can't see the ghosts but knows they're there?" Mom said.

"Maybe. I just got the sense he wasn't telling me something." And who could blame him, really? Why would he owe me any sort of explanation? And it wasn't as if my teddy bear PJs, ratty t-shirt, and slippers were exactly speaking loads about my competence.

Mom got up to make us some hot tea, and I tucked the blanket around my feet stretched out in front of me. It felt good to release myself from the tight ball I'd created of my torso and legs as I had worked to stay warm.

When Mom came back with the tea, she lifted the edge of the blanket, and I pulled my legs back in so we could share it. There's nothing like the comfort of another body under a blanket on a snowy day, especially since the strangeness and the danger—mostly from the cold—I had been in was now hitting me. I was crying quietly, almost before I knew it.

I'd always been like that; pretty cool during a crisis, then prone to intense physical and emotional reaction once the crisis was averted. As I sobbed quietly, Mom ran her hand up and down my calf. Eventually, I quieted, and we sat for a while longer in that warmth.

But it wasn't long before both Mom and I were on the hunt for answers. We grabbed our laptops and set up a research station at the dining room table. Since school was cancelled, Mom didn't have appointments—her therapy practice operated like churches in this way. No school, no client meetings. And so we settled in for a day of Shady Run School story hunting.

If you are white in America, chances are you don't know much about anything but the stories of the most powerful people in our history—the Founding Fathers, the presidents, the Pilgrims, the pioneers, the business tycoons. By and large, these people were white men. Occasionally, school history lessons throw in a bit about Marie Curie or Geronimo, but then, often even that teaching becomes a factoid or the expression someone uses when leaping into something with fearlessness and wild abandon. We are not good at teaching ourselves about the full richness of our history.

So the fact that neither Mom nor I had heard of Rosenwald Schools shouldn't really come as a surprise to anyone. It didn't even come as a surprise to us then. Our experience with Moses and the graveyard a few months back had taught us that we knew very little about the realities of life beyond our own privileged paths.

Thus, learning—or maybe, understanding—that black people in Virginia were not allowed to be educated with white people came as a surprise. Of course we knew about Brown vs. Board of Education, the ruling that abolished the idea of "separate but equal," but neither of us had really thought about what that meant for the people on the unequal side of things. That story only really had meaning for us because of the way it disrupted—and from our place in history, we thought that disruption perfect and good—the standard way that white people lived. The fact that school integration meant a profound shift in opportunity AND in the way people lived their days, yep—never crossed our minds. I know, Mom and I talked about it.

As we began to read about Rosenwald Schools, about how Julius Rosenwald, who owned Sears, gave money to help build schools for African American children in rural areas, we started to get a picture. All children were required, by law, to go to school, and yet, black children weren't allowed to go to white schools. Of course, because it was only fifty years past slavery, most of the money still lived—and still does live—in the hands of white folks. So while white communities could usually scrounge up some dollars to build schools and hire teachers, black communities had a much harder time doing the same thing. Still, with Rosenwald's money, a little county funding, and donations from the members of the local black communities across the state, 382 Rosenwald Schools were built.

It took me some time to really grasp that. But Mom helped. "Think about Mr. Henson from church, Mary." I imagined a smiling, portly guy with a gray beard and short, wide fingers. Mr. Henson was one of my favorite people in the world because he laughed all the time. He laughed at commercials, children playing in the church yard, at the way he dropped things all the time. That man had the best laugh.

I smiled. "Okay. I'm thinking about him."

"Now, imagine Mr. Henson when he was seventeen."

I drew up a picture of him, thinner, but still stocky and broad-shouldered. His hair was dark, dark brown, and he had a hammer in his hand. He was standing in front of a cabinet, sliding one corner into another, his dovetails perfect. (Don't be too impressed. This is the only carpentry thing I know—dovetails.) At seventeen, he had been an apprentice to a Charleston cabinetmaker. He'd told me as much when I'd gone out of church to go to the bathroom and had joined him, instead of returning to the sermon, in his little cubby by the back of the sanctuary where he counted the offering.

Mom looked carefully at me. "Now, imagine that Mr. Henson had been born in 1850, and when he was seventeen, he was just two years out of slavery. He was learning cabinetry, but he didn't have any of his own tools yet, and every bit of money he made— from doing repairs to building rustic farm storage to selling his eggs to his neighbors—he saved to buy land."

In my mind's eye, I saw Mr. Henson's chestnut skin, and when he laughed, the corners of his eyes were creased, his hands cut and sore. Already, his young shoulders were stiff from worry. I let my mind conjure his parents, people who had worked—without earning but a tiny, tiny bit of money—very hard every day at whatever they had been told to do. I saw his mother, her hair already turning white at the age of thirty-five and his father, thirty-nine, his back curved toward the earth he hoed all day for eight months of the year. She worked as a washer with her hands soaked in lye all day and so split and raw in the evenings that she had to salve them with lard. Mr. Henson's daddy had worked a plow for the same man who had once listed him as part of the property with that farm and got only forty-one cents an hour for his labor. I see them greeting their son over a supper of wrinkled potatoes cooked in the fire, and I watch Mr. Henson's mama lay a tiny sliver of bacon on her son's plate. They wanted him to thrive. They needed him to succeed.

"Oh, Mama," I sighed.

"Right, Mary." She looked like she wanted to cry, too. "Now, think about Mr. Henson when you first remember him, when you were a little girl. He was in his sixties, remember? Think of him if he'd been born fifty years earlier. Slavery had ended just fifty years earlier, and he has married and had children, and his children have had children. He's watched his parents die. He's bought three acres of land just a few miles from where his parents and he were slaves. Now, every time he stands up straight, he feels an ache all the way down to his toes."

I shifted in my chair, my hips suddenly very sore.

"His great-grandchildren are now four and five years old, and he knows that they need what he and his own parents were purposefully denied. He knows that they need what their parents couldn't get either. They need an education so that when they are sixty-seven and want to take a walk it doesn't take them a full mile before their backs straighten out."

"So Julius Rosenwald, he gave people not only some money, but he gave them hope, right?"

Mom smiled and got up to make us another pot of Earl Gray. Meanwhile, I stared at my computer screen, an image of a white building, broad and short, in the upper-right corner. Before it, nineteen tiny children stand perfectly still as someone snaps their picture. It's the Shady Run School in 1952, and there is Henrietta, even tinier, standing on the first step of the building.

4.

y the time Mom and I decided to take a break and watch *Buffy the Vampire Slayer* about mid-afternoon, we knew that Shady Run had been built in 1923, that it had operated until 1954, and that it had closed for no reason that we could find.

Other Rosenwald schools were open until the late 1950s and early '60s, when integration became required, but Shady Run closed in 1954—that's what the UVA site said— but it didn't give a reason.

As Buffy slaughtered vampires with her wooden sticks and cheerleading round-offs, I thought about Henrietta and the other kids there. I couldn't quite figure out how that many ghosts get trapped in one space. Ghost theory—believe me, I'd read most of it in the past few months—held that ghosts stayed if they had unfinished business, which was true in my experience, limited though it was. Some paranormal experts also contended that a person's spirit could get attached to a place through traumatic death. That seemed possible, too, but how did thirteen people die in a school? The most obvious option for that kind of mass death was a fire. Yet, the building was still standing and didn't show signs of anything like that.

Eventually, I got wrapped up into the Pee-wee Herman death scene and forgot all about Shady Run . . . the movie turned into a Netflix marathon of Sarah Michelle Geller and Anthony Boreanis, pre-*Bones*, and Mom and I ate popcorn in front of the TV as the snow turned to the tiny bits of powder that means it's almost done.

When I got up next morning, the snow-plows had been through, and I got dressed for school. I liked school, loved it actually, not so much the social part, the part that most teenagers love. I just liked classes itself, the chance to learn things.

But I loved my friends, too. Marcie and Nicole had been dating for a while now, and while it wasn't easy for two women to date in our tiny town, most folks were at least used to it.

And then, there was Javier. I still went all tingly around the back of my shoulders when I thought of him. We'd been together a few months now, and it was still good. He was still good. Sweet

and kind. Yeah, I know, save the mushy stuff for
Snapchat.

I hadn't really given myself enough time this
morning, so I had to forego Mom's grits and bacon
and opt for a lemon Luna bar for the road. I stood
at the edge of the yard and saw the bus coming
around the corner.

Then, I was standing at Shady Run again. At
least I had on a coat and shoes.

This time, I'd appeared in the schoolyard,
and I could see Charlotte and the children inside.
Clearly, school was actively happening. Two of the
boys in the back kept raising a straw to their lips—
spit wads ready—but before every attempted shot,
Charlotte turned and gave them THE stare.

As I watched that peaceful scene, I noticed a
gas lantern on Charlotte's desk and saw that the
walls inside looked brighter. I chalked it up to the
morning light and my imagination and started toward the door. I paused before going in—did I
smell chimney smoke? *Whew, I need more sleep.*
Henrietta came running over and leapt into my
arms as I dropped my backpack to catch her.
"Morning, Miss Henrietta. How are you?"

"I good, Miss Mary. Come play with me?"

I set the small girl down on the floor. "In a
minute." I could see Charlotte in the doorway to
the hall, and the tightness in her jaw told me we
needed to talk.

"You came back?" she said gently as we
pulled out two desks from the corner. If we kept

this up, we'd have the schoolroom back into rows in short order.

I looked around the small room, at the blackboards behind Charlotte's head, and nodded. "I did." My voice wasn't exactly confident, but then, no matter how many times it happens, appearing whole-body into a new place was not really ever going to be normal. "I wish I knew why," I said under my breath.

"Pardon?"

"Oh, nothing." I took a deep breath. "So Micah Tindall . . ."

Charlotte took a breath so deep her shoulders almost reached her ears. "Yes, Micah." She stared at the air above my head, and her eyes lost focus.

I glanced over to see Henrietta and some other children—three girls and two boys— holding a tea party for a stuffed bear.

When I looked back, Charlotte was still lost in thought. "Charlotte?"

She glanced down at my face and gave her head a little shake. "Oh, my apologies. I let myself disappear into my thoughts for a moment there. How very rude."

"No worries." She wrinkled the skin above her nose. "It's okay. Tell me about Mr. Tindall."

"Micah was a smart boy. Really good with numbers. I told him he could go to college, get a job building big buildings for companies in places like New York City." A gentle smile touched her bottom lip. "I can still see his face when we talked about New York. The way his eyes sparkled and his feet danced. The boy never could sit still."

"But then, when he was thirteen, his daddy was killed in a logging accident, and Micah had to start working to help his family. He still came to school, but he was so tired all the time from his night job at the gas station. Most days, I just let him sleep by the woodstove." She glanced over at the corner where a chimney opening went through the ceiling.

"He still did his lessons though, and he was still good at math. So good at numbers. The boy could do long division in his head."

I was trying to imagine the big man who had been so scary to me could be so kind as a teenager. I could get the face smoothed out and thinner, but that body—I imagined those shoulders had been broad forever.

Charlotte took a deep breath and studied my face. After a few moments, her eyes softened, and she began to speak again. "One day, though, Micah came in, and he was so angry. I could practically feel the rage coming like heat waves from his skin. I asked him what was wrong, and he just shook his head. Later that day, I would learn that a man, a white man, had assaulted his sister Marianne when she was on her way home from work at the grocery store. Two of that boy's friends had watched while she was attacked. She got away but not before she was humiliated and terrified."

I felt the anger bubbling inside me, too; the anger for Marianne, at the way a man felt he could touch her, at the way society still lets that happen. I exhaled loudly. I didn't know Micah Tindall well, but I could imagine his rage. It was still written in the cords of his neck.

Charlotte's shoulders fell a little, and she looked down at her hands. She was working that seam in her sleeve again. "After that, Micah couldn't really concentrate. He was always asking me about laws, about punishments for different things, like assault or vandalism." She sighed. "He tried to act like he was just interested in legal studies, but I knew. I knew that boy was scheming, and there wasn't a thing in the world I could do to stop him."

Her eyes shadowed, and when I glanced down, I could see she had wrapped her fingers into knots. I leaned forward a little.

"A couple of weeks after Marianne's attack, Micah didn't come to school. That boy always came to school, even when his fever burned my skin, so I knew something was wrong. I sent Isham down to check at Micah's house, and when he came back, his eyes were as big as plates. That's when I knew."

"It took a while to get the story out of Isham. He didn't want to get Micah in trouble, and he was pretty shook up. But eventually, it came out that Micah was in jail, that's what Lydia, Micah's mother said. The night before, he'd run down the boy who assaulted his sister, hurt the child badly enough that he was in the hospital. Didn't kill him, mind you, but close. Now, he was in jail because the boy's friends recognized his car."

I leaned back in my seat and took a deep breath. Here was a part of the world I didn't understand. If I had been assaulted, the police would have—probably—taken my statement, identified the attacker, and arrested him. The boy would have gone to trial and been tried by people within the system—a judge or jury. But I knew that even now, in 2015, if a young black girl was attacked or even raped, there was a good chance that no one would believe her, that her rapist would get off scot-free. And in the '50s, well, no one was going to go to the "trouble" of tracking down a white boy who attacked a black girl. The girl was obviously "asking for it," that's what girls did, after all, just made themselves available. I'd heard boys in my school say that today.

I could feel the rage crawling up the back of my neck, and I forced myself to take a few breaths. While I didn't like Mr. Tindall's choice to hit that boy with his car, I couldn't judge it either. After all, justice was not something that would have been served for his sister if he hadn't taken some justice for her.

Charlotte stood and smoothed her skirt. "Micah was tried and found guilty. But because he was only seventeen and because the white boy lived, he didn't serve much time—a few months, I think. He did his time without complaint, and when he got out, he went right back to work, just like before. Only now, he was eighteen and too old for school. So I didn't see him much after he was out, just passed him on the road sometimes. He'd always wave, but he never spoke. All of this had broken his spirit, as it would, of course."

She looked so very sad, *forlorn* was the word that came to mind. I felt pretty sorrowful myself. This was the great sadness of knowing history—that you could know it, feel it, even relive it sometimes, but you can't change it. You just have to carry it and hope that healing comes in time.

That story of history, the story of a man I had met, a man who had seen my own plight and shown kindness even when he didn't have to . . . that story was heavy. I tried to remember if I had said "Thank you" when I got out of his car. I couldn't recall, but I sure hoped my manners had kicked in for me.

We sat quiet for a bit longer, Charlotte and I, and watched the children stack blocks in the corner and then kick them down. Some of them sat talking quietly, sharing the secrets of their young lives, I imagined, and others were drawing pictures on the blackboard—I could see their focus, the way those tiny fingers gripped the chalk and moved in circles and squares. But nothing showed up on the board itself, at least not to my eyes . . . whole stories lived in their imaginations, and I was blind to see them.

After a while, I let my eyes drift around the room. The wide planks that made up the floor, the light-green paint on the walls that reminded me of my stereotypical image of hospitals, the windows that took up most of one wall. As my eyes drifted over the windows, my vision caught on something in one corner. A jagged piece of glass hung down there, a tooth of edge dangling.

I pried myself out of the tiny desk and went over to look. I could see close-up that one pane of glass was broken out entirely. In terms of the whole window, with maybe eighteen panes, the hole was small, and since it was tucked into a corner, I imagined most people didn't see it.

"That was the way they got it in." I jumped as Charlotte spoke at my left shoulder.

"Got what in?" I put my finger against the wood window sill and pulled it back dusty.

"The hose. They slipped the green hose into the school that way. I still don't know how they broke the glass without us hearing."

I turned to look the schoolteacher in the eye. "Beg your pardon, Charlotte. But what are you talking about?"

She turned and walked away from me, and I could see her hands hanging limp at her sides. "That's the way they killed us, Mary. Through that little hole in that big window. That's the way they murdered us all." She waved a weak hand over the children still playing in the corner.

All the breath left my lungs. I stared at Charlotte as she walked slowly by each child, laying a hand on a shoulder or a head. *She didn't just say she and these children, children!, were murdered, did she?* I couldn't think straight and leaned my head and shoulders back against the wall.

Then, I pulled myself upright and strode over to Charlotte, stepping in front of her as she walked a slow circle around the room. "Did you say *murdered*, Miss Charlotte?"

She stopped, looked me right in the eye and said, "Yes, ma'am." She took a step to the left and walked around me, continuing her path.

I watched her stroll for a while and then took pace beside her. "Do you mind telling me about what happened?"

She seemed to think this over, letting her head drop just a bit to the right. "I suppose not. I don't know how it could matter. We're dead, after all." She took a breath. "You're just the first person to ask, is all. But then, you're the first person to see us, too."

I kept step with her as we made a full cycle around the room, and then she took a quick look at the children and said, "It was the week after Micah Tindall got out of jail."

"He didn't come to school anymore, of course, but he did stop by to help out sometimes. Some mornings I'd come in and find him by that wood stove," she pointed to the chimney thimble, "a full fire blazing and the room already beginning to warm. He was a good boy, I mean, a good man."

I thought I saw a hint of a blush on her cheeks then. She was really just a girl herself, maybe twenty-five.

"One morning when I found him here, he was really agitated, pacing back and forth in front of the stove so quickly that I thought he might walk through the floor. When I asked him what was wrong, he said, 'I haven't done anything, Miss Braxton. Not a thing. But still, they's coming after me.'"

"I asked him who was coming after him, but he didn't say another word. I convinced him to stay here with us that day, that he'd be safe here. I knew the school was a calming place for him and thought we might be able to talk after classes were done. He agreed and took a seat in that corner." She pointed to the space where all the desks were piled.

"The children began arriving, and honestly, I kind of forgot Micah was here." She let her eyes drop to the floor. "We began our lessons, and I was going on about things when I heard the car pull up. Most of my students walked to school—their families couldn't afford cars—so I was surprised to hear an engine outside. I walked to the window to see who was here and heard the back door close. When I turned around, Micah was gone."

I looked toward the cubby of a hallway at the back of the school and saw light coming through a window above a doorway.

"Just then, Micah came around the front of the school and three white boys—maybe sixteen or seventeen—got out of a car. Micah was walking toward them, and I could see there was going to be a fight. I got the children to the back of the room and had them start reciting their alphabet. I thought maybe that would keep them distracted and drown out the shouting outside."

"I stepped back to the window, and Micah must have caught a glance at me because he waved me back away from the glass. He looked so frightened that I did what he said and sat down with the children in a circle on the floor."

She and I walked back to the corner then. I could picture them, twelve children and their teacher on the floor. I remembered those circles from my early school days. I loved when the teacher was down there with us, reading a book or playing a game. It felt like special time, a moment when the world adjusted to who I was on the planet.

"I decided to read the children a book and picked up Old MacDonald. We've read that book together so many times that the children often shout out the sounds the animals make. Maybe that was why we didn't hear the glass break." She paused and looked at the window.

"After the story, I glanced out and saw that the car was still there. But Micah and the boys weren't anywhere in sight. I assumed that they'd gone off to fight or talk or whatever elsewhere, and while I was worried about Micah," she looked me in the eyes, "you understand I had to worry about the children first."

I nodded. Of course. I'd seen my teachers at school work to break up fights but then hurry back to their classrooms, eager to restore calm. Fights were always disturbing to me, even as a teenager. I couldn't imagine how scary they'd be to a little kid.

"The next thing I knew, I was waking up to the sound of a car pulling away." She took a deep breath. "I looked out the window to see Micah. His face was bleeding, and even from that distance, I could see that one of his eyes was swelling up. He looked up at the window, and I waved."

She wrapped her arms tight around her waist. "He came running toward the building then, grabbing the green hose out of the window as he passed. I hadn't even noticed it until that moment."

I leaned in now, trying to catch her eye as she was staring at the floor.

"When he came through the door, he bellowed like a cow stuck in mud. His eyes were wide, and he threw his hands to the top of his head. He was staring into the corner, so I followed his eyes. That's when I saw us . . . the children and me, all still asleep in that circle."

5.

Charlotte and I talked long that morning. She told me about their first days, how hard it was for the children to understand they couldn't go home, about their wails when their parents came to visit the building after the police had cleared out the bodies, about how she had eventually realized that she was going to be responsible for these children forever.

"I love these children, Mary." She looked me in the eye as she said it. "But I'm their teacher, not their mama." As her eyes grazed the tiny faces in the corner, she whispered, "I'm so tired."

I sat with her until the children grew restless and we could see the pinchy shape of their voices going after each other. I felt older as I rested my hand on her arm before I walked toward the door.

I walked home this time in the shadow winter light of late afternoon. I'd always liked this light, the way it made everything seem slower, as if we were all lizards adapting to the cold air.

Down the hill to the corner and then over to my own street, I looked at the houses I passed. Small, neat dwellings with tiny picket fences around plots of ground that would hold daffodils in a few weeks. I saw lights on in a few windows, faces behind them either oblivious to me or watching me closely. People don't walk country roads much, or at least white girls don't walk the country roads where black people live, not very often.

Now, that's not because of fear, at least not mostly, I think, not like in the city where when I enter a black neighborhood I have to fight the impulse to hit the auto-lock on the car while Mom drives and feel bad about that right away. No, here it's more about the regular old separation of things. White folks and black folks don't live much in the same neighborhoods, even now. That's why I'd never been up this road before, I guess. I didn't feel great about that, though.

I got home about the time the bus would have dropped me off, and so Mom didn't think to come out of her office and check on me. I was starving, so I got myself a big spoonful of peanut butter and headed to my room.

I dropped onto my bed, flipped onto my stomach, and braced my feet against the headboard behind me. Then, I opened my laptop and headed to the library page. Last year, I'd learned a lot about research, and so I knew I had to get some public facts around all these stories.

The Terra Linda library had digital versions of our local newspaper, the *Daily Mountaineer*, and I was looking for the story. I scrolled back to 1954 and started scanning. I figured that the death of a teacher and twelve of her students would be on the front page, so I flipped through the pages quickly, flinging each one to the left when I didn't see the headline. By the time I got to December I was confused—Charlotte had said they were killed in October—but I was also angry, and could feel the heat of that emotion in the underside of my forearms.

I clicked back to the beginning and started over, this time reading every headline in every issue. Finally, I found it on the eighth of nine pages of the paper for October 12, 1954:

Negro Teacher and Students Found Dead In Local School

The article was about three lines long, and it was buried between a recipe for lemon pound cake and a story about the little, white girl who could spell *antidisestablishmentarianism.*

It read:

On Friday, the bodies of the local Negro teacher, Miss Charlotte Braxton, and 12 of her students at the Shady Run School were found in their classroom. Authorities have concluded that a ventilation problem with the wood stove caused the teacher and students to suffocate.

That was it. It was five days later, and the authorities had concluded that a wood stove—a wood stove that worked perfectly well every other day—had caused thirteen people to die, and none of those people had thought to open a window or go get help. No investigation.

The article didn't tell me anything about Charlotte or her students, no mention of funeral services or anything. Just three lines about a curious incident that didn't even warrant a full story.

I spun my body around and screamed into my pillow as hot tears poured down my face.

Mom helped me get some perspective while we ate a dinner of mashed potatoes, canned green beans (my favorite), and some sort of vegan meat-thing that she wanted to try. (For the record, I ate two bites of the vegan thing and three helpings of potatoes. I know nothing if I don't know how to comfort myself with food.)

"So someone killed that teacher . . ." Mom looked up from her plate.

"Charlotte Braxton."

"Right, Charlotte. Someone killed her and her students because another student beat up a kid who assaulted his sister? Horrible."

I nodded. I was still having trouble understanding how exactly it was that thirteen people could suddenly die in a building where they spent hours almost every day and people could think that "natural." But I'd learned recently that trying to make sense of racism was like trying to understand the scattershot run of a squirrel with a nut. There's nothing logical about it . . . just fear, fear running wild and frantic.

Mom chewed a piece of her fakin' bacon and studied my face. Her eyes squinted, and she swallowed. "So what are you going to do?"

This was the question I'd been avoiding for the past two days. I knew I needed to do something—that I'd materialized in that school for a reason—but since I had no clue what to do and was still kind of tired from the last time I'd talked to a ghost, I had been trying to think of other things.

But of course, I had been pulled to Shady Run for a purpose. Micah Tindall had shown up while I was there for a reason. Sometimes God or the Universe or Fate or whatever was not very subtle.

I shrugged. "I don't know yet, but I think it's probably time to get everyone back together to talk."

Mom nodded and stood to take her plate to the counter. Then, she picked up her phone and began dialing. I did the same, standing at the big windows at the back of our house and looking into the forest behind. By the time an hour had passed, we'd talked to Javier, Marcie, Nicole, Shamila, Mr. Meade, and Isaiah, and everyone was on their way over. Friends, the folks who will drop everything when you've seen a ghost.

Within the hour, we were perched around our living room on couches and the floor. Javier and I were leaning against the hearth, our legs just touching, and Mom was sitting on the arm of the chair next to Isaiah. Marcie and Nicole were tucked into one end of the couch, their hands interlaced, and everyone else, all the non-coupled people, were scattered about the room. It felt like home in an even richer way.

I explained what had happened to me over the last two days and passed out printouts of the news article.

"Alright, let me see what I can dig up about the murders. Maybe we have more articles or some letters and things about it," Shamila said. I could picture her already huddled over the microfilm machine at the historical society.

"And I'll see who I can talk to that was alive then. I've met Micah Tindall, so maybe I can even talk to him. Mary, want to come along?" Isaiah asked.

I glanced at Mom, and she nodded. Tomorrow was Saturday, so I wouldn't miss another day of school to get some more answers.

We talked a while longer and set about on some plans to start getting the word out about the murders by passing out copies of the article with a request that people help us investigate. But Mr. Meade urged us to slow down just a little. "Maybe it's best that Isaiah talk to Mr. Tindall first. After all, this story is really his, and maybe he'd rather not drag all this back into the open."

Isaiah nodded. "True. Let's see if I can talk to him this weekend, feel out what he's thinking."

"But Charlotte and Henrietta and those kids were murdered, and now their ghosts are trapped in that building. We can't just do nothing." I was getting heated, and I could feel tears at the back of my eyes.

Mom stood up and walked over to sit on the opposite side of me from Javier, who was rubbing his fingers over mine. "Mary, no one is suggesting we do nothing. But surely you don't want to hurt Mr. Tindall further by trying to do something good without really knowing how he feels about it."

I took a deep breath. No, I didn't want anyone else to get hurt. That was certain, but still . . .

Mom put her face down so she could look in my eyes. "Maybe he can also help us understand more about what happened so that we make wise choices."

I nodded. "Okay. Maybe you and I can try to talk to him tomorrow, Isaiah?"

"Yep. We'll head up to his house in the morning." He stood and stretched. "We'll let everyone know how our conversation goes ASAP. Then, we can get a plan in motion to get some justice."

Javier stood, then reached down to pull me up. "Are we the Terra Linda justice league then? If so, do we need tights?"

I had an image of each of us in brightly colored leggings and let my mouth turn into a smile. The visual of Mr. Meade in green tights lingered into my dreams. It wasn't pretty.

The next morning, Isaiah and I stood outside a low-slung, long, white house just a few doors up from the school. As we'd driven by the schoolhouse, I'd gazed into the windows and saw Charlotte with her hands out from her sides looking out over the classroom. She was teaching something, I realized, and I wondered—not for the last time—how she filled fifty years of days with lessons to children who never got older and who never graduated.

Mr. Tindall's house was tidy and well-kept, with boxwood hedges trimmed flat in the front and two white rockers on the slim front porch. His car was in the gravel driveway, and through the front windows, I could see a wooden table with a bunch of silk flowers on it. I looked at Isaiah, and he nodded, then walked up the concrete front walk.

It didn't take long for Mr. Tindall to answer; a few paces, I imagined, given his long legs, and as I stood back by the car, I saw he and Isaiah shake hands before Isaiah turned to look at me and wave me to the porch.

"Hello, Mr. Tindall," I said, suddenly feeling very shy and having to fight the impulse to stare at my shoes. I wasn't sure what was going on with me, but I forced myself to look him in the eye and say, "Thank you again for the ride home the other day."

"My pleasure." He said it like he meant it but also in the way that Southerners say lots of things we mean out of politeness but don't really put much force behind.

"Micah, we were wondering if we could talk with you for a minute," Isaiah said.

Mr. Tindall stepped back in the doorway and let us pass. His house was exactly like I'd imagined it—clean, spare, comfortable—but I hadn't imagined that his walls would be covered with neatly-framed pictures of children. As far as I could tell, Mr. Tindall wasn't married. He didn't wear a wedding ring (I double-checked his finger), and I didn't see a second car in the driveway or hear anyone else in the house. Maybe his wife had died and these were the children they'd had before she passed?

Isaiah and I sat down on the light-blue sofa, and Mr. Tindall lowered himself into a wing chair that was covered in blue-and-brown plaid fabric. Then, he looked at us out of the tops of his eyes.

Normally, I wasn't shy about starting conversations. In fact, I typically leapt into words without thinking twice. It was a habit that got me into trouble, and the people who loved me knew that. So on the way over, Isaiah had gentled that it might be best if I let him talk first, go in a bit easy. He didn't have to say it, but I also knew that it was important that Isaiah talk first because we were bringing up a subject where white people had done horrible things, and while Mr. Tindall certainly wouldn't lump me with those terrible boys, it was just respectful for the black folks to talk about this first without having to deal with my privilege, too. At the time, I probably couldn't have articulated it that way, but I knew it, even still.

"Micah, Mary and I were wondering if we could ask you about the school, Shady Run."

Mr. Tindall's glance flicked to me and then back to Isaiah. "What do you want to know?" His shoulders were stiff, but he also leaned in just a bit.

"Well, we did a little research and read about what happened in 1954 . . . to the teacher and her students."

Mr. Tindall collapsed back against the seat. I couldn't tell if he was relieved or exhausted, maybe both. "Terrible days. Those were terrible days."

I settled back against the sofa a little more and waited.

"You know, those boys never got in a bit of trouble for killing thirteen people. Not a bit. Not even a talking-to by the police or the mayor or anybody. That's what you call scot-free." His hands were trembling where they sat on his knees.

Isaiah said, "We read about that, and it's awful. Absolutely awful. So awful, in fact, that we were wondering if it would be alright with you if we tried to bring some justice here."

Mr. Tindall leaned forward real slow. "Why you asking me that question, Isaiah?"

Uh-oh.

"Well, Micah, I've heard that some people think those boys did that terrible thing because they were mad at you. Now, I certainly understand why you did what you did, and I know you served your time. So our concern is not with you but with justice for that teacher and those children." Isaiah took a deep breath. "Plus, well, I don't know what I would have done if someone had assaulted my sister. I may not have had your restraint."

Across the small room, Mr. Tindall let out a heavy sigh, and it felt like the roof lifted off of us for a second but then settled back on even heavier. He looked at me, and I tried to smile, but I expect my lips didn't turn up at the corners.

"And you, Miss? Mary? That's your name, right? I know you did that work with the cemetery last year, and that was a good thing, but I'd think you'd be tired of getting into this old business by now."

I looked the man in the eye and straightened my shoulders. "No, sir. 'A threat to justice anywhere is a threat to justice everywhere.'"

Mr. Tindall let out a roar of a laugh, and I couldn't help but smile. "Child, you're quoting Martin to me? Ain't that something?" He stood up. "Can I get y'all some tea? I expect we're going to be talking a while."

6.

While Mr. Tindall was in the kitchen, I slipped my notebook out of my back pocket and into my lap. Isaiah gave me a small nod. Last night, we had talked about whether we should ask Mr. Tindall if we could record him but decided that might be too much for this first conversation. Instead, I said I'd ask if I could take notes.

So when he came back in with three mugs, each with the logo from a different bank in town, I asked, "Mr. Tindall, would you mind if I take some notes on what you say, just so we remember the details later?"

He set the mugs down on the coffee table between us and looked into my eyes as he sat down. "On one condition . . ."

I braced myself for some condition about not telling anyone or doing anything with the information. I really wanted to be able to take some action here.

"You have to call me Micah." His jaw loosed a bit, and I saw a tug of a smile at his lips.

"Deal." I uncapped the pen and got ready to write.

Most of what he said was exactly the same as what Charlotte had told me, but he added a lot more detail. He told us that when his sister was attacked, she wasn't just assaulted; she was raped and then beaten so badly that she had a broken shoulder blade and six broken ribs.

I sucked the air back against my teeth. No wonder he had gone after the men who attacked her.

When he got to the morning that Charlotte and the children were killed, his voice got softer, heavier somehow, and I had to lean forward to hear him.

"I just went by that morning because I missed it there, I guess. I'd always loved going to school, the learning, and the books. But I also really liked being somewhere that I had to only do one thing. I didn't have to worry about walking the wrong way or looking someone in the eye by mistake. I didn't have to always push myself to the back behind other people." He leaned back in his chair and looked out the front window.

I wasn't sure how to relate here, how to find my way into this experience. Never once had I been expected to step off the sidewalk when someone else was coming toward me or had to wait in line because someone of another skin tone was, by default, waited on first. But I knew this was what Micah was talking about. That had been his childhood reality. I'd read about Jim Crow in books—about the separate water fountains for white folks and black folks, about the lunch counters where college students were spit on for wanting to order a hamburger like anybody else—but to hear someone talk about his experience of living it, well, that was enough to make my heart feel ragged.

"When I heard a call pull up, I looked out the window and saw them there." He looked up at us. "The boys who had attacked Marianne—and I knew we were in trouble. I figured if I went out to meet them, they'd take me and do whatever they wanted. I couldn't let them get to Miss Braxton and the other kids. But when I went out there, I could see it in their eyes. They weren't just after me. They'd come to do something big, something that would make them feel important. They caught my eye and looked right past me to the school, and that's when I knew. I charged at them, trying to stay quiet so the kids wouldn't get scared, but trying to scare those white boys away, too. I made myself as big as I could, and I told them to go home. That no one here wanted any trouble. They just kept staring at the school. I looked back and saw Miss Braxton in the window. I tried to tell her to get back, and I saw her look of fear before she turned back to the children." He let out a shuddering sigh.

"I took a step toward the boy closest to me, but I didn't get far. One of them must have hit me with a baseball bat because that's the last thing I remember. When I came to, they were gone."

I could picture this teenage boy, a huge black eye and his head swelling up, as he looked around. I could imagine that he thought everything was okay, that he almost smiled . . . until he noticed the silence in the school.

"There wasn't a sound coming from that building. Not a laugh. Not a murmur. Nothing.

Then, I saw the hose. I ripped it from the window as fast as I could and ran for the door, but it was too late."

I imagined Charlotte seeing him come into the school, hearing his wails of grief and rage, and as I sat here on Micah's sofa, I saw him, too, felt his screams rumble against the inside of my throat. I had to take a huge gulp of tea to keep from crying.

"They were all there. Dead in a perfect circle in the middle of the room."

The images of all those mass suicides by cults came to mind. But here, people weren't fooled or brainwashed into death, as awful as that is. No, these people, these children were murdered. My hands were shaking with rage.

He told us about how he called the police, about how one new deputy came out to the school, took a couple of pictures, and wrote down only a fraction of what Micah said. "Six words. He only wrote down six words. I counted." He left without even bothering to call the coroner to come get the bodies.

"I had to go get some of the men in the neighborhood, and they helped me get all the bodies to the church next door. We laid everybody out nice and pretty, and then we called the parents." Micah swallowed hard. "The screaming in that building that afternoon . . ."

What would my mom have done if she'd come to our church to find my body? What would she have done if she'd learned I was murdered and there would be no investigation? I expect someone in that police department would have been held down by the throat, but then, my mother was a white woman, and if she threatened someone, she didn't have to worry that the police would come and arrest her—or worse—everyone she loved.

I put my notebook beside me and let my head drop back against the top of the sofa, my throat bare and raw.

Just then, the front door slammed open and a man stomped into the living room. He had the same build as Micah. Sharp lines carved the sides of his mouth as if he'd been holding a scowl for decades.

The man looked at Isaiah and then he saw me. If it was possible for eyes to narrow to knives, his did. "Micah, who are these people?"

"Darren, they're new friends. This is Isaiah, and this is Mary." Darren didn't make a move toward us. He just stared, but what my friend Tina calls "home-training" kicked in, and I stood up to shake his hand.

"I'm Mary Steele." I held my hand out as steady as I could make it, and eventually, he shook it one time and hard enough to strain my shoulder. I kept my smile steady, but it hurt as I sat back on the sofa.

"They're here asking about Shady Run, and I'm telling them the story."

"Why you want to know about that?" Darren wasn't talking to me, though. He was looking hard at Isaiah now.

"We read about the story in an old newspaper," I could tell Isaiah was making sure not to look at me, "and we were just curious, is all. It's just terrible that thirteen people die and no one does anything."

I thought Darren's shoulders relaxed a bit, but I still found him very intimidating. "Yeah, yeah, it is terrible."

"I was telling them about Marianne and . . ."

"What they need to know about that for?" Darren was shouting this time, his face inches from Micah's. "That's none of their business. You need to know when to stop talking."

Isaiah and I stood up at almost exactly the same time, and he said, "Darren, we mean no harm, and we're not trying to pry. That's why we're here. We wanted to get your brother's permission before we started doing more research about what . . ."

"Research. What research you got to do? There's nothing more to know. Some white boys raped our sister. Micah tried to get some justice when no one else would. Then those same white boys killed that teacher and those kids." His voice was so loud that it was hurting my ears now. "Ain't nothing good going to come out of stirring up this trouble again. Nothing."

"Darren, why you here?" Micah asked in a gentle voice. "What do you need?"

Beneath that question I thought I heard decades of brotherhood, one man trying to help the other, of bearing patience like a shield.

"I just came back to borrow your car to go over to Lexington."

"Sure." Micah took a set of keys out of his pockets and tossed them the inches to his brother's hand. "I don't have to go anywhere until church tomorrow."

Darren clenched the jagged keys in his fingers and looked hard at Isaiah and then at me. "Nothing good come out of this curiosity, you hear me? You best leave it alone."

This time, though, his voice was softer, more pleading. I knew that voice. It was the one I used when I was scared.

Isaiah nodded once, and Darren turned and walked out the front door. We heard the car door slam and the engine start, and I'm fairly sure all three of us let out a big breath then.

"Don't mind Darren. He was little, just nine, when Marianne was attacked and Miss Braxton and those kids were killed. He should have been one of them, but he was home sick from school that day."

I could almost hear Mom's voice say, "Survivor's guilt." I nodded and leaned forward to put my elbows on my knees. I was suddenly very, very tired.

"So afterwards, the police didn't do anything at all?" Isaiah asked in a gentle voice.

"Not a thing. We had funerals for a full week after that, and the whole community turned out." He paused and looked at me and then back at Isaiah. "The black community, I mean. And then, that was it. No one said a word after that, not the police, or even reporters. We talked about it quietly at church, tried to figure out if there was something we could do. Darren wanted to go after those boys, and several adults agreed with him. But in the end, we knew that nothing we did would bring those children back, and any action would just come back to hurt us worse in the end. I knew that firsthand."

I saw pools in Micah's eyes then, and I had to swallow hard again myself.

Isaiah looked at me, and I nodded and then stood. It was time to go.

"Micah, do you mind if we do some research about the murders of Miss Braxton and the children? We don't want to make trouble for you." I saw Isaiah's eyes trail to the door that Darren had slammed shut behind him. "But we feel like justice isn't being served here, and Mary, well, Mary feels very strongly about wanting to do something."

I looked Micah in the eyes and took a step forward. "I don't know if you will be able to believe this, Micah, but I didn't choose to show up at your school." His brow furrowed. "I didn't walk or drive over there two days ago. I just appeared there. That's why I was in my pajamas."

Micah turned his head and looked at me out of the corner of his eye. "You just appeared there?"

"Yeah. It's something that happen to me. I can't control it." I took a deep breath. "But when it happens, I've learned it means I need to do something, that something is wrong."

Micah looked down at his hands and then met my eyes again. "Okay, Mary. Let's do something. But you really have to tell me about this 'just appearing somewhere' thing." He took a breath. "Another time, though."

I smiled. *Here we go*, I thought.

My smile faded quickly, though, when I saw Darren Tindall in his car, glowering at me as Isaiah and I left.

7.

"The gang's all here," I said as we perched again by the fireplace in our living room. I'm not even sure where that phrase comes from except that it has that tint of cliché that makes it comforting.

Isaiah quickly told them what Micah had told us, and I shared Darren Tindall's warning and told them about him watching us from his car when we left. Mom shot Isaiah a quick look, and I saw him squeeze her knee. They were worried, too.

Mr. Meade sat forward from his seat on the couch and said, "It's still early enough in the semester that I can get another research group started."

I started to say that I'd be happy to take folks to the library and show them how to use a microfilm machine when Mom spoke.

"I don't know, Tom. Do we want the kids . . ." she glanced at Marcie and me by the fireplace and then over to Javier in a bean bag next to me, ". . . investigating murders that happened just a few years back?"

Javier sighed. I could almost hear his thoughts. *Why does everyone always underestimate teenagers? We can do so much more than you all let us do.* But I knew he wouldn't say anything. That wasn't his way. He spoke when things needed to be said, but more, he was a man of action, quick to help when a direction was set.

But I felt frustrated, too. We weren't new to racism after all, and if anything, a mystery involving people who were still alive might get our friends really excited.

Wait, people who were still alive? The people who committed these murders were probably still alive. The realization hit me like a wave and stole my breath. We weren't talking about killers who were long dead, people who lived in stories and gene pools. We were talking about real-life people. People we probably knew.

Mom must have seen understanding come to me as I sat there slack-jawed because she said, "Mary, you see what I mean, right?"

I let a long breath out through my nose. "We could be researching our friends' parents."

"Right. Your friends' parents, or the clerk at the grocery store, or the man at the Exxon who plugged your tire last week."

I shivered. *That man had been so nice. It wasn't possible, was it?*

I felt Marcie shift beside me. "I would feel better if we did this research quietly, maybe with Shamila at the Society, rather than in big meetings." Her voice was quiet but firm, and we were all listening. Marcie was not a scared person, not at all, but I could hear a tremble behind her words.

"I'm happy to put together a research plan and bring in a couple of trusted volunteers to help," Shamila spoke. She had been writing down everything in a marble-covered notebook perched on her knee. Now, from the barstool she'd slid over from the kitchen, she talked her way through what we could do.

"First, we need to find out exactly what the police reports say about Mr. Tindall."

"Got it." Stephen Douglas stood from the couch and headed for the door. "I'll scan the files and get them over to you later today, Shamila." Police connections did have their privileges.

"Be careful, Stephen," Isaiah said. "Some of those officers may have more at stake than just negligence."

Stephen nodded as he slid on his coat. "See you all later." He looked at me. "Text me about when we're getting together again?" I nodded and sighed a little prayer that no one would really notice him at the station on a Saturday afternoon.

"Next, we need to go through the old newspapers and see if there's any other coverage. Maybe expand our search out to Lynchburg and Roanoke?"

Nicole leaned away from the fireplace. "We can do that." She looked at Marcie, who nodded.

"Great. Mary, since you know the school best, maybe you could ask Micah to take you over there and explain what he saw." Shamila paused. "Maybe Charlotte, too."

As the rest of the group took assignments—Mom and Isaiah to ask around town about what happened and Mr. Meade to create a series of lessons about Rosenwald Schools as a more neutral research project—I wondered how I'd manage to talk to both Micah and Charlotte at the same time. I didn't know how Micah would take to the news that Charlotte and the children were still there, if he'd be frightened or feel guilty. Maybe both. I didn't know whether to tell him or just find some way to disguise that I was listening to Charlotte, too. Whew, this was going to be a challenge.

The group broke up to begin their research after we set a plan to meet back here on Tuesday night to see what we'd learned.

I told Mom I was headed over to Shady Run to look around. "Be back by six. We're having pizza and watching *Dead Poets' Society*." I knew this was a deliberate choice, a film to remind me that Charlotte might have been like Mr. Keating.

I slipped on my pea coat and walked hand in hand with Javier over to the school. "Man, this is all something," he said as he rubbed his thumb against my hand, soothing in his quiet way.

"Yeah." I paused and stared at the skeletons of trees along the road. "Can I tell you something?"

He stopped and turned me toward him. "Of course. Always."

"I'm kind of scared." I almost whispered the sentence. I didn't want anyone else to hear. "I mean, this is murder. Kids were murdered." We started walking again. "Mary, if you weren't scared, I'd be worried." Javier slipped his arm around my waist and pulled me against him. I let out a long sigh.

When we got to the school, I walked up the front stairs and tried the door, expecting it to be locked, but it swung right open. So we went in. I didn't see anyone in the building, except Charlotte and the children of course, and I scooped up Henrietta as she ran full-tilt to me.

That's when I heard a gasp from the corner. Micah stood by the pile of desks facing me, and he could clearly see Henrietta now. Or at least I thought he could because he was staring right at her face, and she was staring right back.

"You can see me, Mr. Micah?" she squeaked in a tiny voice as she pulled her knees tight around my hip.

I moved my gaze from him to her tiny, frightened face.

"Miss Mary, can he see me?" I thought she was going to cry.

I took a few steps toward Micah, and he bounded back and crashed in the desks. Yep, he could see her.

I glanced first at Javier and then over to Charlotte and saw the muscles in her jaw clench before she met my eye and nodded. We met each other in the center of the room, and I took her hand.

Micah let out a loud gasp. "Miss Braxton." His voice sounded younger somehow; maybe it was the awe, maybe the fear.

I let go of Charlotte's hand, and she walked slowly toward Micah. "Yes, Micah, it's me." She reached him and laid a gentle hand on his forearm. "We've been here the whole time."

His knees went out without a sound, and Micah crumpled into a heap on the floor with his eyes fixed on Charlotte's face. She knelt down beside him and met his gaze level. They stayed like that for a long time, and one by one, I moved among the children, touching them gently on a shoulder or running my fingers along their cheeks until I knew that Micah could see all of them.

Slowly, Charlotte helped him to his feet, and he looked around the room. Tears rolled gently down his cheeks, and then almost as if he had fallen again, he knelt down and opened his arms, and the children ran to him. Henrietta wriggled out of my grasp and piled in, too, and I wondered if just this act of grief and grace might be enough to set them all free.

After a few minutes, they all turned to me where I stood by the front window, and I knew it was time to explain. So I told them how I sometimes showed up at places where ghosts were, that I didn't understand how or even really why, but that I knew it was intended by Someone and that it meant—at least the last time—that I needed to do something.

Micah, Charlotte, Javier and I pulled desks to the center of the room, and Charlotte settled the children into a corner while one of the older kids read them *The Cat in the Hat*. I told them all about the last time and about my friends, about how that was why Isaiah and I had come over to Micah's house to get his permission. Then, I told them about our plan to get more information, to see what we needed to know.

When I was done, Micah and Charlotte looked at each other, and then she said, "Mary, that's very kind. But this is dangerous. These are dangerous people."

"Bud Granger still owns the Exxon, Mary, and Merle Popson works for the water department. Last I heard, Stu Tomlinson still drove a school bus, too. These people are still here, still working and living and worshipping alongside us, Mary, and I expect they aren't going to take too kindly to folks stirring up trouble." Micah's brow was folded with worry.

I looked down at my fingernails and contemplated sliding the white of my pointer finger between my front teeth, but chose instead to say, "We know. We know this could make trouble."

"Not just trouble, Mary." Micah interrupted me. "People could get hurt."

Javier put a hand on my back, and I let out a hard sigh. "We know. I know, but Stephen Douglas, from the police department is working with us, so he'll . . ." I trailed off when I looked at Charlotte's face. It had gotten as hard as stone. *Right, the police hadn't done anything before.* I took another long breath. "I know. But Stephen, he's a good man. He really is."

A glance passed between Micah and Charlotte again, and she nodded. "Okay, Mary. But you have to let me help."

I felt my heart rate quicken a bit. "Really? Okay. That's great." I glanced back at the children still reading behind me and smiled.

"But before I help," Charlotte said, "I want to meet everyone involved. I need to look people in the eye and see their faces. I expect you understand, right?" She looked over at Micah.

He nodded.

"We can do that. Tuesday night, maybe we can meet up here so you can talk to everybody." Charlotte looked at me out of the corner of her eye. "Oh, they know about you already. They kind of get this ghost thing with me. It doesn't worry them."

Micah let out a sharp snort. "Well, good for them." Then, he looked at me and winked.

8.

The next two days flew by as I squeezed in every bit of research I could between classes. I had sent Shamila the names of the men who had attacked Micah's sister and killed Charlotte and the children, and she was looking up any information that might be found about Bud Granter, Merle Popson, and Stu Tomlinson in the Society's records. Stephen was pulling police reports, and Javier, Marcie, Nicole, and I spent a good bit of Monday evening spinning through microfilm looking for their names.

Meanwhile, Mom and Isaiah were doing a little "recon." Mom had used that word about twenty-five times before breakfast on Monday, and I had this vision of her and Isaiah in black, knit caps and black jumpsuits rappelling into the gas station to get intel. Every time I felt the fear prick the back of my neck, I pictured Mom hanging horizontal over the Dunkin' Stix and Ho Hos, and I felt better.

By Tuesday evening, we were all set to go to Shady Run and met at our house to carpool. As our small coalition gathered on the lawn, milling like fish without a school, I felt like I maybe was supposed to give some sort of half-time, locker room speech to send us forth with determination. It felt like we were going into battle, but I didn't feel much like inspiring. The silence of our research was too heavy.

So far, we had discovered only one mention of Granger, Popson, and Tomlinson in all our digging, a simple note in a police record that said the boys had been questioned at their home and didn't have "anything to add to the investigation." I snarled as I remembered the word *investigation*. Does a cover-up really count as one?

I wasn't looking forward to telling Charlotte and Micah what we'd found—or rather what we hadn't found. How does a person stand up under the weight of silence around her murder? I'm not sure I could, but then Charlotte had been caring for twelve children for over sixty years. Clearly, she was a stronger person than I.

We drove over to the school in two cars, doing our best to keep a low profile. We'd brought flashlights and a couple of camping lanterns to light up the building while we were there, but we'd also brought some blankets to drape over the windows first. No need to draw attention to what we were doing. Stephen had let the office on patrol know that he was going to be up at the school that night because he'd seen lights up there, and so no need to worry if someone called in about seeing someone there.

We parked Stephen's cruiser and Marcie's mom's minivan by the school and quickly made our way inside. I walked over to Charlotte as soon as I saw her and touched her arm softly. Marcie's gasp was the only sound in the room. I suppose it would be startling to see someone appear out of nowhere. I wouldn't know. The children came close then, and I laid a hand on each shoulder before scooping Henrietta up last.

I could tell Mom and Isaiah, Mr. Meade, Javier, and everyone else could see them now, because there was a sadness etched into their faces—a sorrow at seeing the spirits of dead

children. The reflection of their grief brought
me near tears.

Nicole and I spread out some blankets as
others covered the windows and lit the lanterns, and soon, all twenty-one of us—living
and dead—sat in a huddle in the middle of the
schoolroom floor. The children snuggled
against Charlotte and me, and one little boy
with spheres for cheeks climbed into Isaiah's
lap. Just then, Micah came in, and his smile set
his sadness into relief. He eased himself to the
floor with us.

Shamila began to fill everyone in. "I'm
sorry to say we didn't find much. A few church
bulletins from congregations near here at
Shady Run mentioned your, um, services."

She looked at Charlotte, but Henrietta
said, "We know we're dead. It's okay."

I glanced down at the sweet face laying
against my chest and marveled at the wisdom
of almost seventy years tucked into a little
body.

"Well, then, yes, the bulletins talked
about funerals for all of you." Her voice softened, and she looked at each child in turn as
she said, "Your parents and brothers and sisters were very, very sad."

"We know," a little girl with tight corn-rows and purple beads at the tips said. "We seen them when they came to visit."

"Saw," Charlotte corrected. "We saw them."

The girl, whose name was Joan, squiggled her nose. No one likes to have their grammar corrected in public.

Shamila smiled and continued. "But we couldn't find anything beyond mentions in the newspapers here or in Lynchburg or Roanoke. It seems like people didn't really know about your deaths."

"Oh, they knew," Micah said quietly. "They knew, but they didn't care. Or if they cared, they couldn't do nothing—I mean, anything—about it." He glanced at Charlotte. "That was just the times."

Mr. Meade spoke up. "Yes, it was, but it's not those times now, and we're going to make sure people know about what happened to you."

I saw a look of alarm pass over Charlotte's face, and Mr. Meade spoke quickly. "We aren't going to go around accusing anyone, not without some evidence, of course, but we want to help people remember you. We have an idea."

"It'll keep the story of your deaths in front of the police while we work to see what evidence we can find about your murderers," Stephen added.

The energy in the room had lifted, like hope had streamed in with more oxygen.

"We're going to do a fundraiser to fix up the school and then commemorate it in your honor," I said before quickly adding, "if that's okay with you, Micah."

We hadn't told him about this idea before, afraid he'd say no on impulse, but as I looked at him, I realized we'd underestimated him. "I love that idea," he said, the emotion graveling his voice. "What do we need to do?

"Well, first, we need some money," Mom said. "So this weekend, we're going to—with your permission—hold tours of the school. We want people to see the building, to know what's here, to understand its history."

Isaiah added, "We'll have to do a little work for that, of course. Be sure the stairs are solid and handrails safe, and maybe clean a little, but nothing major."

I looked over at Marcie, and she was staring at the broken window where it peeked out from behind an old quilt Mom had tossed over the window. "But we don't fix that. Not yet."

We all looked at the window. Nope, that would stay broken.

The next few days were a flurry of work at the school. Micah gathered retired folks who had attended Shady Run, and they did a massive clean-up of the school building and the yard. Dead trees were taken down, and old shrubs removed. The blackboards that surrounded the classroom almost shone. When they were done, the building was pristine; still run-down, but clean. Now, someone could come and see what could be done to save the building without being distracted by dirt.

Marcie, Nicole, and Javier made a short video about the school—with Darren and some of the school's graduates—and we laid it over the guitar track of a local musician who agreed to let us use his work. Then, Mom got to work with Isaiah and created a crowd-funding campaign, complete with giving rewards, including stickers, mugs, and t-shirts that a local company had printed with the sketch Mr. Meade did of the school.

I wrote to all the preservation, genealogical, and historical organizations in our area and some in Richmond, too, and let them know about the school and about our crowd-funding campaign.

If we could make a film montage of our lives, this would have been a *great* montage sequence.

Within a couple of weeks, we had raised $10,000. *The Roanoke Times* had done a story on the school, and Micah had given an interview for them. An organization called Preservation Virginia had added this school to their list of Rosenwald schools and was helping us get the word out about our work, and the local community—particularly folks from the black churches—had rallied. It felt like it had taken no work at all to get that $10,000, but of course, we were doing the hardest work more quietly.

Shamila and a couple of volunteers that had grown up in Terra Linda had started an oral history project related to the school. They were recording the memories of people who had gone there—any memories they wanted to share. But with each interview, they included two questions: What do you remember about the teacher, Miss Braxton? And what did you know about her death and the closing of the school?

One woman said, "Miss Braxton was a good teacher. Kind of strict, but really good. It was terrible what happened to her. You can't rightly keep a school open when a teacher and twelve children die in it, now can you?"

"I probably shouldn't be saying this," a ninety-two-year-old man said, "but that teacher and those kids, they didn't die by no accident. No, someone killed them, filled that building with carbon monoxide and let them turn blue with it. But then, that was the way then. Might still be the way now."

With gentleness, Shamila tried to get more information, push for names or more details, but mostly people were general in their talk— "trained," Shamila said, by decades of silence.

9.

We had a powerhouse of work. The older men led the charge in all things, as was only right since this was their story we were exploring, their history, and Isaiah and Mom were their footmen, foot people. What is the gender-neutral version of that term?

While the rest of us were at school or work, Micah, Isaiah, and Mom took to some mighty work. They hung posters and contacted legislators. They met with county officials and held interest meetings in churches and at the county retirement home. Within a week, they had garnered the interest of a few hundred people—both white and black—in the Shady Run school. I had managed to write a B+ paper for Mr. Meade and eat five pieces of cafeteria pizza. Clearly, I was not the star of this show, and mostly that was okay. Mostly.

I kind of missed my press conferences. For a little while.

We also got to work on fixing up the school. We needed to work on the driveway and get some landscaping done, refinish the floors inside, get the interior painted, and put together a plan for how the school would be used. Micah was certain he wanted it to be a community center—he'd seen that other neighborhoods were doing that in their Rosenwald Schools—so he and Isaiah were working on a business plan for how to make that happen. Meanwhile, we all agreed that we needed to get the outside of the school looking good as quickly as possible so that people could see progress was being made. Nicole's brother Tyrice painted houses on weekends, so we hired his crew to begin. And that's where the trouble started.

On the first Saturday they were set to begin work, it was twenty-eight degrees. February is not the ideal month for exterior painting in Virginia, of course, but the guys—all six of them—had a lot of scraping and patching to do to the wood, so they figured they could do that for a few Saturdays until it got warm enough to paint. They were there, all bundled up in Carhartt jackets and knit caps, some on ladders, and some bent to scrape the wood near the ground. Mom and I were inside washing the walls and talking with Charlotte when we heard the cars pull up.

I glanced out the window, expecting to see Javier and his friends, who had planned to come to help, too, but instead, I saw a bunch more guys from school, guys I knew. In a school of 500, there isn't really anyone you don't know? I didn't like them though. Well, except for one. Blanch was there. He saw me at the window and tossed up a limp wave.

Uh-oh.

I turned to Mom, who must have seen the look of alarm on my face, because she dropped her rag in the bucket and met me at the front door. Already, the new guys were in the faces of Tyrice and his crew, and I could see this might get ugly quickly. I ran out the door to Blanch, who was standing under the oak tree at the corner of the building. He looked angry, really angry, but since he had arrived with the guys who were stirring things up, it took me a minute to realize he was angry at his friends. When I touched his arm, he flinched away. "Oh, sorry, Mary. I didn't see you."

"It's okay. What's going on, Blanch?"

He let out a loud sigh. "Popson over there." He pointed at Dave, a senior with a penchant for throwing scorn at everything but football and the final school bell. "He wanted to come over and see what was going on. Told me that people were messing with the school, that we might need to stop them."

I looked closely at Blanch, and he finally met my eyes.

"Sorry, Mary. As soon as we pulled up and saw Tyrice, I knew that Dave had lied. He's just doing what his granddad wants." Sometimes, I'm not all that bright, it seems, because it was only in that moment that I realized Dave Popson was Merle Popson's grandson. If it wouldn't have looked ridiculous, I would have bonked myself on the forehead.

"Oh. So, do you know what his grandfather did?"

Blanch's face flushed. "Yeah, Dave's been bragging about it since last night. His granddad told him about it when he saw the article in the paper."

Yesterday's paper had a front-page story about the school and Micah's efforts to fix it up. It also contained a paragraph about the deaths of Charlotte and the children. Shamila had talked with the reporter and mentioned that was a major reason why the school had closed. She didn't make any accusations—we weren't ready for that yet—but we thought it time to get the word out to see what shook loose. And here we were, shaking racist idiots loose from the high school hallways.

It was my turn to sigh. "We need them to go home, Blanch. Can you help? Or do you think I should call Stephen?"

He looked over my shoulder at his friends. "Let me see if I can talk to them."

We walked together over to Dave and the other three guys: Chris, Ricardo, and Biff. Doesn't every school have a guy named Biff? I knew them all, had known them since kindergarten, and they weren't bad guys as guys go. Just a little bored in our town, a little too enamored with the idea of being rednecks. Ricardo even had a Confederate flag that he flew in the bed of his pick-up truck, but I knew that he didn't think that was racist. Just Southern.

I also knew it was still racist.

Blanch stepped between Dave and Tyrice, who were just inches apart by now, and Tyrice caught my eye. I smiled, and he gave me a nod and walked back to the building. I caught a glimpse of Mom in the doorway. She had her phone in her hand, but she was waiting.

"Let's go, Dave," Blanch said.

"Nah, I want to know what they're doing. Why are they fixing up some old school?" He took a step toward the school door, toward my mom.

Blanch stepped in front of him again. "Let's go."

I saw Mom lift the phone to her ear and then looked back to Dave. His jaw was locked, and his eyes burned.

"Man, let's go." Biff spoke this time and gave Dave a punch in the arm. When Dave turned around, Biff used his chin to point to Mom.

Blanch shot me a glance, his eyebrows raised, and they all climbed back into the truck and drove off, kicking gravel against me, Tyrice, and the building.

I felt my shoulders drop. "That was close."

"Very," Tyrice said as he pointed over my shoulder. Darren Tindall was pulling up in the schoolyard just then. Two minutes earlier, and I'm sure blood would have been spilled in that schoolyard.

Darren slammed his door— hard—and strode over me. "So you're doing it after all? After I warned you? You just can't mind your own damn business, can you?"

I felt Mom's arm brush against my shoulder. "I'm Elaine Steele. You must be Darren Tindall. I've heard so much about you."

If you're not familiar with Southern speak, you might not know that my mom had shown Darren that she knew the lay of the land with that one phrase. See, in the South, if someone says, "Oh, it's a pleasure to meet you. I've heard only wonderful things," then you know that people have been speaking kindly to others about you. But if someone says, "I've heard so much about you," it's only politeness that keeps them from saying, "I hear you're a real ass."

Darren looked Mom in the face and shook her outstretched hand down once before dropping it. His gaze then lifted to Tyrice, and then spread across the building. I could have been mistaken, but I thought I saw his shoulders lift under his heavy coat. *Ah, he likes it after all,* I thought.

I didn't really want to say anything, but politeness—and maybe a little smugness, too— dictated I give him a tour. If Micah had been there, this role would have fallen to him, but since I was the one leading things today, the duty fell to me. "Would you like a tour?"

"Girl, I don't need you to give me no tour of *my* school."

"Oh, I'm sorry. You're right. So right. Would you mind giving me a tour of the school then, maybe tell me what you remember?" Geez, politeness didn't get me far in the face of anger.

Darren harrumphed but headed toward the front stairs. I shot Mom a "come get me in ten if I haven't come out" look and followed him inside.

As soon as we got in the door, I saw Charlotte take hold of Henrietta's shoulders so the child wouldn't leap at me like usual, and I gave the teacher a gentle smile. It wouldn't do to be talking ghosts with Darren, not just yet, at least.

Since I'd been here pretty much every day since that first time I appeared, the change in the building wasn't that shocking to me, I guess, but Darren's jaw hung slack as he walked slowly around the perimeter of the room. He ran his hand along the chalkboard frame and took steady strides past each window until he stood back by the door.

"I have a wood stove that would fit in that corner." He spoke so softly I almost hadn't heard him.

I smiled. "That would be great. We're trying to take the building back to the way it was in the '50s. Is there anything else you remember?"

"Miss Braxton always made the room colorful. She had flags from around the world on the wall and the pennant from Jackie Robinson's Dodgers over there. That wall was saved for the little kids' drawings, and her desk sat over here. It was always so neat." His voice was getting softer, wistful, maybe.

"Do you remember how the desks were arranged?"

He didn't answer but strode toward the lines of desks against the back wall. Within minutes, he had the room lined up like a classic American painting. All the desks, except one, faced the place where he said Charlotte's desk had sat. The one remaining was in the back corner opposite the wood stove, and it faced the wall.

"Time-out corner?" I asked.

Darren smiled. "Well, we didn't call it that then, but yeah. I spent a lot of time staring at that wall. I wonder . . ." He walked over and bent down low. "Ha! Wouldn't you know it? It's still there."

I walked over, and he leaned back so I could see. Just by the corner, about waist high, the initials DT were carved into the plaster.

"I got bored," he said and smiled again.

I could see Charlotte over his shoulder grinning and shaking her head. "I found that a few years back, and I knew it was Darren. That boy always had a good heart and a huge temper. Seems like times haven't changed much."

It felt like we were on steadier ground now, Darren and I, so I took a little risk. "Mr. Tindall, so what do you think? Can we bring back this building? Make it the community center that your brother wants?"

He scowled at me and then surveyed the room again. Then, his expression softened once more. "I suppose so. But Mary," he looked me in the eye with something that seemed to be concern, "some people ain't going to be happy about this, you know that, right?"

"Yes, sir. Some of those unhappy folks were here before you got here."

He frowned.

"But Mr. Tindall, there's things a whole lot worse than unhappy. There's dead. And it's time that Miss Braxton and those children got some justice, don't you think?

Darren turned toward the broken window and stared.

10.

The next day after church, we all gathered at the school, and Mom and I told everyone what had happened.

Tyrice was there, too, eager to help with more than just painting, and he told us all that he'd run into Blanch at Hardee's the night before, and Blanch had apologized.

"For a big boy, that man has a tender heart," Tyrice said, and I smiled. I loved Blanch, maybe not in the way he wanted me to love him, but I loved him nonetheless.

"Seems like word is already out just about the building, and people are getting squirrely," Mr. Meade said. "I'm not sure if that means we should go ahead and announce that we're going to call on the police to reopen the investigation into Charlotte and the children's murders, or if we need to keep it even more quiet."

Stephen was sitting in the corner with a little boy on his knee and Henrietta leaned up against him. "My instinct is that we need to wait to make any public announcement in that regard until we are sure the police department will act. It's one thing for people to get riled up about rumors and another altogether for them to start doing things to protect themselves or the people we love. I've seen buildings burned down for less."

"You don't think they'd burn the school down?" I almost squeaked.

Isaiah looked at me gently. "Mary, you know these people, the ones who want to hold onto their hate. You know they're capable of most anything, right?"

"We've started patrolling the school at night, just to make sure no one is up here messing around," Micah said. "Some of the men from the neighborhood and I."

"And we send a patrol car around on every shift." He looked at Micah. "The chief owed me a favor."

Javier spoke from beside me. "Maybe we should put up a camera, too, just in case. One of those game cameras that will take pictures if there's any movement. I have one we can use if you want."

I looked at my boyfriend out of the corner of my eye. What was he—drummer, video-game lover—doing with a game camera?

He must have caught my look because he said, "My grandfather's store was being vandalized, so we got one to catch the culprit." He laughed. "Turned out to be my ten-year-old cousin, mad at Abuelo for not giving him candy every time he asked."

"So then, what's next?" Mom asked.

"I have some information you all might want to hear," Shamila said. "I've been looking through the Historical Society's records, trying to find anything I can about the murders." Every time one of us said that word we whispered because the children were in the room. "Charlotte, do you, did you, um, have a sister?"

"Yes, ma'am. Lucille. She was three years younger than me."

I suddenly had the image of a young woman who looked much like Charlotte but fleshier, more earthbound somehow.

"But then, I guess now, she'd be an old woman."

My imagination aged that woman, gave her some wrinkles in the places that connote wisdom, let her flesh hang down a bit more.

"Right. Yes, Lucille. In the '80s, she came to the Society to find out more about the history of the school. Our notes say she was hoping to go visit, but at the time, we couldn't find out who the owner was. She told the director then that she was going to be looking into her sister's 'murder.' That was the word she used, and she wondered if the Society could help her find anything about the incidents of 1954. She knew about your sister, Micah, and about your time in jail. She said her sister had told her. But she didn't know any specifics."

I looked carefully at Shamila's face as the corners of her mouth turned down and her brows dropped. She was angry.

"But our director then told Lucille that all this was just a dust-up when some people forgot their place, that she didn't know why Lucille thought these were murders instead of sad accidents, but that there wasn't anything more she could do."

It felt like the oxygen went out of the room. Racism carried a profound silence with it everywhere.

"The director's notes said, 'Told that schoolteacher's sister that it was all an accident. Felt there was no need for outsiders to get mixed up in private town business. Called Merle Popson to let him know someone was asking questions.'"

Marcie leaned way in. "She knew."

"She did," Shamila said. "Everyone knew, I think. And no one did anything."

The weight of breathlessness settled around us as we all took in what we suspected but hoped was not true. People had deliberately hidden the fact that Charlotte and these twelve children were murdered because they wanted to protect their friends, their white friends. But more, of course, in some ways, they thought Charlotte and her students were expendable, worth less than the image of a quaint mountain town, and certainly worth less than the lives of the boys who killed them.

My mouth tasted bitter.

"I did find one thing though, Charlotte." Shamila handed Charlotte a slip of paper.

"Lucille Braxton Clough, Norfolk, Virginia."

"Your sister was living in Norfolk then, and we know her married name. Maybe it's worth us making a visit to see if she's still there."

"You mean if she's still alive," Charlotte said. "Let's speak plain here. She may be dead. Just like my parents are dead. Maybe my brother, too."

As if the weight of this history couldn't get worse, a young woman realizes that her entire family may have died without her knowing it. I tried to imagine what I'd feel like if I was away and couldn't get to my mom in her last days. I felt tears well up in the bottoms of my eyes.

Micah stood and walked behind Charlotte, laying his hands gently on her shoulders, and I saw a shudder pass through her. How awful it must be to carry such grief and not be able to let it out because you are the sole caretaker of twelve children's souls.

After a few moments, Nicole stood up and said, "Road trip to Norfolk?"

Charlotte glanced at her and said, "Maybe you could take a camera so I can see her if she's there?"

I smiled. We could do one better.

The next day, Mom, Nicole, Marcie, Javier, and I were in Mom's minivan on the way to Norfolk. Our plan was for Marcie, Nicole, Javier, and I to talk with Ms. Clough about the school under the guise of a school project, which wasn't really a lie because Mr. Meade was letting us do our term papers on the school.

We had a tripod that his band, the Screaming Lizards, used to shoot videos for YouTube, and Mom had just upgraded to the latest iPhone. We'd film the interview—and here was the best part—livestream it back to Micah and Charlotte at the school. Charlotte didn't know a thing about that bit, and I was thrilled that Shamila had agreed to film Charlotte's reaction, if we could catch Charlotte on film.

We drove past all the war ships at the Navy base and traveled on to a little community of neat, tidy houses all in a row. Ms. Clough's was the third on the left, and the front porch was lined with boxwoods. On the porch, she had a porch swing and a big flowerpot, which was empty in the winter.

I went first and knocked on the door. Three solid but respectful knocks. I hated when people banged; it was just rude. It took a while, but I finally heard rustling coming from the back of the house, and soon, a tall, white-

haired woman in a velour track suit and pearls
came to the door. "May I help you?"

"Ms. Clough? My name is Mary. I'm
hoping Shamila Harris from the Terra Linda
Historical Society called you to tell you we
were coming."

"Oh yes, please, come in." She pushed
open the storm door and showed us into the
cutest—and also maybe the creepiest—room I
had ever seen. It was lined with dolls, ceramic
dolls that stood waist high and wore velvet
dresses and trailing stacks of curls. I couldn't
help but stare and soon found myself walking
around the room to look in each doll's face.
Some of them were boys and some girls, some
white, some black, some brown. I was particularly taken with a doll with long, blonde braids,
a plaid shirt, and overalls.

Ms. Clough watched me stop at the overalls doll and said, "That's Cassie. She's one of
my favorites." She gestured to a sofa and two
chairs, and we sat. "These are my babies. I
know some people think it's a little weird for a
grown woman to collect dolls, but I just love
them." She turned in her seat across from me
and pointed at a tall, African American doll in
the corner. "That's Bea. She's my favorite."

I looked from Ms. Clough to Bea and back. "I can see why," I said and smiled. Ms. Clough and Bea were in exactly the same outfit, and I could see some of Charlotte in the doll's fine cheekbones and high forehead.

"Yep, I had her made just for me. If I couldn't put my genes into a flesh-and-blood human being, I figured at least I'd have some likeness of me that would last after I was gone." She paused and winked at me. "See, told you people think I'm a little weird."

I laughed out loud. I liked Ms. Clough already.

We talked a few minutes as Javier got the camera set up, and we told her about our project, about how we were hoping to preserve the school and fulfill Micah's dream of turning it into a community center.

"Micah Tindall! I haven't heard that name in fifty years." Her face shadowed a bit. "So he's still living?"

"He is, and he sends his regards." *His regards.* I don't say things like that normally, okay? It was a little awkward there in this part of the morning.

"That poor man," Ms. Clough continued, and I gave Javier a nod to start filming and saw Marcie and Nicole take out their notebooks.

"He had a hard, hard time of it after Marianne was attacked."

"Can you tell us a bit more about that, please? Oh, and it is okay if we film our conversation?"

"Yes, honey. That's fine. Well, Marianne was attacked by three teenage boys one afternoon after school. No one talked much about it, so I don't know how bad she was hurt. But the police didn't do a thing." Her voice got deeper and harder. "Not one thing. That wasn't rare in those days, in these too, from what I hear, but just because it was normal doesn't mean it hurt any less. After all that piled-up hurt, a person can lose some perspective, even a God-fearing person like Micah Tindall."

"That boy should have known better, but he was just a young man then, I guess. Still walking around with all his ideals shiny and new. Still, I wish someone would have stopped him."

Shamila had reminded us a few times that when recording Ms. Clough's story, we needed to listen far more than we talked. So when Ms. Clough paused, I had to really resist asking about two million questions that were zooming through my head. I took a breath and sat back.

"The night he was arrested I was at church, and I still remember when my friend Helen leaned over and whispered that Micah was going to jail for beating up those boys. We were singing 'Nearer My God to Thee.' As word spread through the church, the singing got louder and louder." She stared out the window, and I followed her gaze to a bird feeder hanging from a low branch. Cardinals flitted back and forth. "By the time we finished the last verse, the church felt like it would lift off its foundation. If singing could bring justice, we would have rained it down that night."

I let out a sigh. I wished singing could bring justice. I really did. Then and now. I'd sing my way through the day if it would help Charlotte and Henrietta and those other children.

Ms. Clough looked at me again. "But when Micah came home, it was just the same. Like Marianne had never been attacked. Like Micah hadn't gone to jail for something white boys would have just been reprimanded for. Mary, you'd have thought that would have broken our spirits in that neighborhood then, but I guess we were too tough or broken already because nothing changed much at all."

I don't know what my face looked like, but I tried to share what they call a *wry smile* with Ms. Clough. I didn't know what else to do.

She looked at the camera and then back at me. "Oh well, I guess there's not much they can do to me now. Might as well tell it."

I felt the hair on the back of my hands stand up. I was tingling. This was it.

"So when those boys put that hose into the school window and killed Charlotte and those children, I think we had all been expecting something. Now, don't get me wrong." She looked from me to Marcie to Nicole to Javier to Mom. "We would have done something if we'd known what was coming. No one was going to stand for the killing of innocent people. Children, Lord, the children." She put her hands on either side of her face, then let them drop heavy into her lap. "But we didn't know. Didn't imagine it would be that extreme. I think we thought they'd vandalize something, maybe even burn the church down one night when we weren't there. But murder. None of us imagined murder."

"Still, when word got out, I can't say as we was surprised."

I couldn't help myself. "So you knew what had happened? You knew who had done it?"

"Oh yes. We knew. Those boys—that Popson, Granger, and Tomlinson—they'd been trouble a long time. Harassing kids downtown. Throwing rocks at black folks' houses. And then after Micah, well, we didn't have any doubt who had done it. And of course, Micah knew since he was there. He didn't tell folks, of course. That would have just gotten him killed along with Charlotte and the children. But he did tell the preacher, and the preacher made it be known in a gentle way."

I must have looked upset because Ms. Clough leaned over and put her hand on my arm. "There really was nothing we could do."

"Couldn't you protest? Or march? Or something?" I had forgotten all about the fact that this was an on-camera interview now.

"Honey, this was 1954, the Civil Rights Movement hadn't even started yet. Sure, we could have marched and staged a formal protest. But what good would it have done? In our little town with the police already showing their sides in the matter."

My jaw was tense, and my knee was bouncing.

"Come sit by me, Mary."

I stood up without thinking and sat down. "It's hard for you to understand. You're white, and it's 2015. But black folks just didn't have any power then. We really couldn't do anything without more people getting hurt or killed." She looked up at Marcie.

"I understand," Marcie said. I looked up at my best friend and realized, yet again, that I did not know this core part of her, this part of her that was shaped by racism, that happened because white people like me had created systems that oppressed black people like her. I felt like I was going to cry.

Ms. Clough put an arm around me, and I felt both comforted and guilty. Here I was, asking a woman about her sister's murder, and she was comforting me. Still, I leaned into her a shoulder a little.

Nicole spoke. "Ms. Clough, can you tell us a little bit about your sister?

At that question, the old woman's face lit like a birthday cake with all of her seventy-six candles. "Charlotte was my favorite person in the whole world. She was smart and funny and kind. This one time when we were little she found a baby bird that had fallen out of its nest and brought it home. Most children would have put that bird in a box and forgotten to feed it so it would have died. Not Charlotte. She mashed up worms with our daddy's hammer and fed that baby six times a day. She took that thing to school and kept it in her desk in a tiny box so she could take care of it."

Ms. Clough smiled. "Do you know that we had that bird—Peepy—for six years? He went everywhere with Charlotte. Just sat on her shoulder."

"Charlotte never told . . ." I almost slipped.

"I'm sorry," Ms. Clough said.

"I mean, I had never heard that about Charlotte before."

The woman gave me a look and said, "Well, I expect there's a lot you haven't heard about my sister." A mischievous grin spread across her face.

From the corner of my eyes, I could see all of us lean in. This was going to be good. I wondered what Charlotte was thinking about all of this as she watched back at the school. I imagined she wasn't thrilled with the turn the conversation was taking.

"Once, when Charlotte was about ten, she took our neighbor's bicycle and rode it into a mud bog so deep that only the handle bars were sticking out. That boy was bullying one of the littler kids, and Charlotte wanted him to know she had her eyes on him," Ms. Clough laughed, "and she wanted him to get that bike out of the bog. We could barely stay in our hiding spot in the tree above it from our laughing at how he kept falling into the mud as he pulled and tugged."

She was taking ragged breaths from laughter now. "Then, once, when Charlotte liked a boy—Tim was his name, I think—she shimmied out a limb by our upstairs window so that she could drop into the bushes and sneak out to see him. But when she slid across the branch, she left a big black stain from the maple sap on the front of her new dress, and then when she dropped into the bushes, she fell in dog poo. So she didn't go on her date, and she had to make up a story about sleep walking to get Daddy to let her back in the house. I was at the stop of the stairs, and I could have rolled down them with laughter. Charlotte was not pleased."

Her stories went on like this for a good while, and by the time she was done, all of us had tears rolling down our cheeks because Charlotte had been a riot, a trouble-maker.

When we all caught our breath, Nicole said, "Do you know what made her want to be a teacher?"

Ms. Clough took a deep breath and said, "Oh yes. She loved school and was good at it, too. She got good marks, and she was always trying to learn more. But out in Terra Linda, the schools for black children stopped at eighth grade, so Charlotte convinced our parents to let her take the bus over into Lexington so she could go to the Lexington Colored School there. The bus cost money, but Charlotte worked on nights and weekends as a seamstress, mostly mending clothes, to make the money. So our parents couldn't really say no."

"By the time she finished eleventh grade—we didn't have twelfth grade then—Charlotte had decided on being a teacher. 'Lu,' she said, 'I'm not sure I'm good at much else besides making trouble for myself, but I'm good at school. I figure I'll be a teacher then, help some other kids get their way ahead, and maybe keep some of them out of trouble, too.'"

My mind flashed to Charlotte's distress over Micah's absence from class, the way she seemed to feel guilty that she wasn't able to keep him from beating up those boys.

"School was a way out for us." Ms. Clough continued. "I don't know if you all can understand it. But it was hard enough to get a job and keep safe in those days. And if you wanted more, like Charlotte did, if you wanted to do more than work a low-paying job as a janitor or maid, then you had to do more. You had to stay out of people's vision, white people's vision, you understand." She looked at me gently. "And Charlotte did that. She got her education without making a fuss and then took her teaching certificate quietly in Richmond. Then, she took over our own school when that teacher moved on to Roanoke."

She took a deep breath and looked down at her hands. "But Micah Tindall, Micah couldn't do that. He just couldn't stay in the shadows, not when it came to his sister, and so there he was in the spotlight. And that light shined on a lot of other folks, too, including Charlotte."

We all sat quietly in that tidy living room, and I thought about how I always believed that being in the spotlight was a good thing, that if people paid attention to you, you were doing something right. And yet, Charlotte, Charlotte had needed to work quietly, to keep her work almost secret just to be able to do what she loved, something that helped other people. What a screwed-up world.

"I don't harbor any ill will for Micah Tindall," Ms. Clough said quietly. "I expect that man has suffered enough without me—or anyone else—heaping guilt and responsibility on him. No, the people responsible for my sister's death and the death of those twelve children are those three white boys." Her face fell, and I thought she might cry. "But I expect we may never see justice for that."

Javier caught my eye and nodded.

"Well, actually, Ms. Clough. We may be able to help a bit with that."

On the ride home, we were all very quiet. I didn't know just what was going through everyone else's minds, but I couldn't help thinking about Charlotte and that bicycle in the mud and about her sister's face, how alike they looked, and how Charlotte would never get to have wrinkles or gray hair. Somehow, I was sadder than ever.

But when we got back to the schoolhouse about dusk, I didn't have time to wallow anymore. A firetruck was in the parking lot, and Stephen and Micah were standing by the driveway, and they didn't look happy.

"What happened?" Mom shouted as she ran toward the building, which was still smoking a bit.

"Someone threw a beer bottle filled with kerosene and a burning rag through the window," Stephen said.

Javier shook his head. "A Molotov cocktail. We live in the Virginia mountains, not Los Angeles."

I had only taken one step from the car before it felt like the weight of the building was going to fall over on me. So I stood there, staring at the tendril of smoke—so beautiful, in a way—spiraling into the dusk.

Micah's face was ashen, and his hands were shaking. I glanced around for a chair to hand him, but we'd long since cleaned up the debris that people dump off at old buildings they think aren't loved anymore. So I walked over and slipped my arm through his and led him to sit next to me on the concrete steps that led to the front door. We leaned into each other as we sat down.

"Do you know who did this?" I almost whispered.

He let his chin drop one time.

11.

The damage inside was minor, another broken pane of glass just above the one the hose had been slipped through—I couldn't help but wonder if that was more than happenstance—and some charring on the floor. Somehow, the flame hadn't caught the nearly-one-hundred-year-old wood on fire. Stephen thought the bomb maybe wasn't made well, but I could see boot prints near the scorch marks and ash on Charlotte's shoes.

When I got to be alone with her for a few minutes, I looked at her out of the corner of my eye and said, "You put the fire out."

She didn't turn to look at me. "I did."

"How?

"I'm not sure. But I knew I couldn't let these children be destroyed again."

I swallowed hard so has not to cry and reached over to grab her hand and give it a quick squeeze. She smiled a tiny bit.

On the report Micah gave to Stephen, he said he'd been driving by on his way home from the IGA when he'd seem a gray sedan leave the parking lot. He didn't get a make or model because people had been stopping by a lot lately, taking a look at things. He thought it was just another curious Terra Linda townsperson. But then he had noticed the smoke and ran to the door. "By then, the fire was out and there was only smoke." He paused a moment and stared at the windows.

"What, Micah?" Stephen prompted.

"Oh, it's nothing. Just thought I saw someone, is all."

Mom widened her eyes at me.

We were standing in the schoolyard again, a clump of people unsure what to do and unable to stay inside because of the kerosene smell. Isaiah was on his way with some cleaning supplies.

"It was Charlotte," I said. "I saw her footprints. She doesn't know how she did it, but she couldn't let the school burn around those kids, not after all that's happened."

Micah turned and looked up at the window where Charlotte stood with her hands on Henrietta's shoulders.

"No, I suppose she couldn't," he said.

It was a late night, that one, as we scrubbed the kerosene and scorch marks out of the floor as best we could. We used an old toaster box to tape up both broken window panes now, and we set up a couple of lanterns that Isaiah got from Walmart so that if anyone was in the building, anyone alive, that is, people across the road would be able to see them. Then, we took some solar lights and charged them with the flashlight Mom had in her car before setting them up all around the building. It wasn't much, but it's what we could do without electricity. We'd work on that come Monday.

When Mom and I got home, we collapsed on the couch with two spoons and some Ben & Jerry's Chubby Hubby. I was frightened, just like the last time someone had vandalized a place I loved, but this time my fear wasn't shutting me down.

As I stabbed my spoon in to dig out another peanut butter pretzel, I imagined myself confronting Dave Popson in the cafeteria, pinning him against the wall with one finger and giving him a lecture that would make him pee his pants.

See, I knew that sedan Micah had described. I could see it plain as day with the "Warring's Ford" sticker on the back bumper and the little dent in front of the driver's side door. That was Popson's car. He'd saved up all his money cutting grass to buy that car from the used car lot at the edge of town when he turned sixteen. He'd bragged about it for days. It wasn't much, but he loved that car just like most of the kids in Terra Linda. Cars meant mobility and freedom and something to do.

I must have been making a pretty intense face because Mom put her hand on mine when I slid it into the pint again. "What are you thinking about?"

I flashed my eyes up to meet hers. "Nothing. Just upset about today."

She pulled her legs up onto the couch and turned to look at me.

"Mary Steele. Don't you lie to me. That is not your, 'I'm so sad' face. That's the face you put on when the movie character won't tell the truth even though that would be for the best. That's your angry face."

"Right, yeah, I'm angry. Shouldn't I be?" I heard the edge of defensiveness in my voice, but I couldn't stop, it even though I knew it would mean a longer conversation than I felt like having tonight.

"Of course you should be, but anger needs to be channeled the right way, Mary. You know that. You can't just go off half-cocked."

I threw my spoon onto the floor. "You mean like Dave Popson did when he threw a burning bottle into a school? Like that kind of half-cocked?" I stood up and strode around the room. "So I'm supposed to stay calm when someone tries to destroy a place I love, a place where people I love live and care about. I'm the one who is supposed to be calm when some-one threatens me and the people I love. How is that fair?"

Mom set the ice cream on the table be-hind the couch and folded her hands in her lap. "It's not fair."

"So see . . . see, you know then. You know they deserve to have something happen to them." I could feel the tears pouring down my face now.

"They do, Mary. They deserve to be arrested for arson. They deserve to have a trial. They deserve punishment." She took a deep breath. "But not by you. You are not the purveyor of justice here."

I stared at her, unable to believe what she was saying. How could she possibly think that Dave Popson would ever be punished when his dad and his friends had killed thirteen people and had never even gotten questioned for it? "You know that's not going to happen, Mama. You know it. I can't believe you trust the system to do what's right when it hasn't done that for forty years."

"I know, Mary. I know. But what choice do we have?"

"We have the choice to do something. We have to do something."

"And what do you want to do, Mary? How do we get justice here? Burn down the Popson's house?"

Her words cut through my rage as I imagined Dave asleep in his bed, the curtains beside him on fire. I felt, for just a second, the sweetness of that, and then a wave of nausea washed over me. I collapsed onto the couch again.

"No," I rasped. "No."

Mom slid over and wrapped an arm around my shoulder. "We'll get him, Mary. We'll get them all, but the right way, the just way. Maybe even the merciful way, okay?"

I looked up into her eyes and nodded. I didn't feel very hopeful just now. Anger was easier than despair.

The next day, Sunday, everyone gathered at the school, and Darren joined us, too. I expected him to be rageful like I had been the night before, but instead, he was very calm, cold, almost, and that scared me . . . a lot.

Isaiah had, apparently, been up all night because he looked haggard, the way a president looks at the end of his or her term, like he'd been wrestling with things too heavy for him to fight alone. He had put up easels, each covered in a towel and waiting to be displayed. I was so tired that I got the giggles as I imagined this as an episode of *Shark Tank*, and all of us were the funders for Isaiah's big dream. I had to stuff my fist in my mouth when I imagined giving Isaiah one million hairbands as venture capital. It was going to be a long day.

As we all settled in on the floor or in the desks around the room, Isaiah began. "I have a plan. I'd like for us to try a healing circle with everyone who had ties to the events of 1954."

I felt my brow furrow. I didn't know what a healing circle was, and from the looks on everyone else's faces, I could tell they didn't, either.

"A healing circle is a process where people come into a space together to listen and to share their experiences. We use a talking stick," he held up a magic wand that looked remarkably like the one Mom had given me when I was eleven and obsessed with Harry Potter, "and everyone gets a turn to speak. We set a time limit for each person's turn, and we keep going around for a set period of time."

He looked at each of us. "I know. It sounds a little hokey if you haven't done it, but I did one at work when we were having a major dispute between management and the floor crews. It really worked because I wasn't sitting there formulating my next answer or trying to get my words in. I knew my turn would come, so I listened, and waited. It helped."

Mr. Meade stood up. "I think this process is similar to some of the American Indian traditions I've read, right?"

"Yes, similar. Here, we'd just add a couple of elements that are special to the discussion of racism. One is that someone can say 'Ouch!' if what another person says is hurtful to them. Then, the conversation turns to them so they can express what was hurtful."

I imagined a whole series of ouches, some shouted, when Granger, Popson, and Tomlinson began to talk and wondered if we'd get anywhere at all. That was, if they'd even come.

"Then, we'd also have a mediator on hand in case two or more people in the circle needed to talk things through more directly. There's a mediation team at VMI—a black man and a white woman—who have said they'll be available if we decide to move forward."

A silence settled into the room for a moment, and then Darren spoke up. "It'll never work. First, no one will come. Secondly, if they come, I'll probably end up killing someone."

A sigh filled the room. I knew what he meant.

"Getting people to come is definitely going to be hard." Isaiah turned to one of the easels and pulled off the towel. "That's why I think we have to couch it in terms of a community forum about the school."

Micah spoke up. "I don't want those people's input about what to do with the school."

Another sigh from Isaiah this time. "I know. I don't really, either, but just hear me out, and then maybe we can try a circle to talk about the idea. Would that be okay?"

Isaiah went through his plan to bring in Preservation Virginia to talk about options for restoring the school, to have Mr. Meade's students do a presentation about the history of the school including the tragic deaths—"Murders," Darren added—of Charlotte and the children. There would be an open house in the school with food and music, and we would invite reporters.

Well, more specifically, I would invite reporters. It seemed Isaiah's plan hinged on my willingness to act—with Micah—as the spokesperson for the event. The thought was that my previous success with the cemetery might garner the event some cachet.

I looked over at Micah. He was staring at the broken window pane. "What do you think, Micah? Are you okay with this?" My voice shook a bit as I spoke, and I felt like I would cry. There was a lot weighing on this idea, not the least of which was Micah's need to put his most deep wound into the public view—deliberately, this time.

He stared a while longer, and then his gaze traveled to Charlotte, who was sitting a few feet to his right with the children at her feet. She smiled at him, and then he turned to me. "I think it's a good plan." His voice was very quiet, but it felt like the room had thundered.

I didn't know if Isaiah's plan would work, but Micah's agreement felt like a blow for justice already.

We began our now-usual course of action that afternoon when we issued a press release about the event, which would take place next Friday night. We thought Friday might be an ideal day if we made it an event. Our friends would come out because it was a safe activity in a town that had almost none, and their parents might come out of curiosity.

The event's title was "A Night to Remember," which Mom said reminded her of her prom, which probably wasn't a bad thing. Mostly, we wanted to stir up the folks who had reason to be anxious, and we figured memory was something a lot of folks wanted to avoid doing, about Charlotte and the children's murders, but also about what it was like here in Terra Linda then.

We billed the event as a historic preservation fundraiser and invited people to come tour the school, learn about the plans for its restoration, and consider a donation to help fund the project. All of that would be happening, but the central piece of the evening's events was a healing circle that we'd planned to introduce after we gave the brief overview of the school's history.

I was having a really hard time imagining how we were going to get people to spontaneously sit down and share their experiences of one of the most horrible events in town history, but Isaiah kept reminding me that most people would take any opportunity they could to really be heard. I was still skeptical. And nervous. Really, really nervous.

But on Tuesday, I got a bit of distraction. Javier grabbed my hand as I headed toward the bus and steered me toward his car in the lot. "My mom . . ."

"I already called her. She knows you'll be home for dinner."

I let out a long breath and smiled.

When we got to the car, he took the scarf I use to hold my hair out of my face when it's not in braids and tied it as a blindfold around my eyes. Then, he put his hand on my shoulder and gently helped me sit down in the passenger seat.

I knew better than to ask where we were going. Javier was a man of few words, and he also had more willpower than I did. If this had been my idea, he would have known where we were going before we took ten steps toward the parking lot.

The car started, and we wound our way back into the mountains. I could tell that much from the motion of the car.

As we drove, he reached over and took my hand, gently rolling his thumb across my knuckles. I felt my shoulders relax. I really did need a break.

After a few minutes, I heard the crunch of gravel, and the car came to a stop. Javier opened my door and led me, still blindfolded, up a trail that was narrow enough that I could feel the tips of branches on my shoulders.

We walked uphill a few minutes, and then Javier turned me away from him and stood behind me to remove the blindfold. When I opened my eyes, I could see all of our town below. It looked tiny, smashable by a giant's foot. But it was beautiful, too. The sparse skeletons of the trees around and below us set the town in relief, and I could see the roofs of all the buildings shining in the late afternoon light.

"It's beautiful," I said. "So peaceful."

"I thought you needed to remember that Terra Linda is home, that it's your safe place."

I leaned back into him and stared. "Yeah." I stood for a long time, my back warming against his belly in the cold winter air. "From up here, you can forget that thirteen people were murdered and their murderers went unpunished."

Javier took my shoulders softly and turned me toward him. "No, Mary. Up here, you don't forget that. You just put it in perspective. Even when the world is brutal and ugly, it's still peaceful and lovely, too. You have to remember that. Otherwise, the ugliness will eat you alive."

I gave him a tiny smile and turned back to the view. Man, I hoped he was right.

12.

By Friday afternoon, we had built a good buzz about the school gathering. The local news had run a story about the school the night before and had even put up a photo of Charlotte and talked briefly about the "deaths," as they called them, that had shut the school down.

Marcie had sent me a text late Thursday night. "Don't read the comments." So of course I did, and then, as usual, wished I hadn't. I'll never figure out why people think they can be so ugly and ignorant online. From the look of the comments on the station's website, most people were none too happy about how the station had "stirred the pot" about what was "ancient history."

Mr. Meade had gotten permission for all his students to leave school at 1:00 p.m. so we could help get Shady Run ready for the open house, which was scheduled to start at five o'clock. Most of our classmates just used the time to cut out for the mall in Lexington, but a couple dozen came on out to the school and helped us hang the photos that Shamila had found in the archives and blown up to poster size. Each time I looked at one of them, I felt tugged, pulled back into history a bit. Images are powerful things.

We hung helium balloons by the turn off the main road and then again at the entrance, too. It's easy to miss a turn in the country, and we didn't want anyone to have an excuse that they "couldn't find it."

Mom and Isaiah had spent their evenings that week putting together a revolving slideshow of images of all the alumni of the school that they'd been able to find. In some of the images, a younger version of Micah's face smiled out at us; Darren's, too. But it was Henrietta's image that stopped me cold as I set up borrowed chairs in the classroom. She looked almost the same as she did now, but a little younger. The difference between then and now, of course, was that she was alive then.

The ghosts I'd met didn't look markedly un-
dead or anything, but their complexions didn't
change, no rosy tint that floated to their cheeks
when they were excited or angry. Their pallor
always stayed the same. But in this image,
Henrietta's face was aglow with laughter in the
midst of what looked to be a great game of tag.

I had to take a deep breath and concentrate on the chairs. It wouldn't do for me to
start crying before people showed up.

The first people to arrive were a black
family, two older men—maybe Micah's age, a
younger couple, and two pre-teen kids, a boy
and a girl. Micah greeted them from his stool
by the door, and then Isaiah took them on a
tour of the building. I watched them as they
moved through the room, the two older men—
brothers?—pointed out the wood stove in the
corner, and I saw the kids laugh at something
they said. As the group made its way around to
where I was manning the punch bowl, I heard
one of the older men say, "This is the chalkboard I had to clean every day."

"HAD to clean? Man, you begged to
clean the board. You was trying to be Miss
Braxton's favorite."

Charlotte and the children were in a space that we'd arranged to mimic the classroom setup— a few children's desks and her desk at the front. We'd thought it best to give them their own space where it was unlikely people would walk through them. Charlotte assured me that it wasn't unpleasant when someone passed through her—"like a warm breeze"—so maybe it just creeped the rest of us out a little.

She was watching the two men as they led their family through the school. I made my way over to her, and being careful to not look as if I was talking to someone, let her tell me about the two men, Randall, who was called "Sweet," and his brother, Reuben. "Sweet always was a bit of a kiss-up," she said with a smile.

Before long the room was full, and I was completely preoccupied with filling translucent plastic cups with sherbet-gingerade punch. So I missed when the ruckus started, only catching on to a problem when I saw the flash of blue lights outside. I made my way through the crowd to the door just in time to see Stephen Douglass step between Darren and a white man about his age. Micah took Darren's arm and led him inside while a woman grabbed the other man's hand and led him a few steps away.

"What happened?" I asked Stephen when he came by the punch table a few minutes later.

"Stu Tomlinson. That's what happened."

"So he came?!"

"Yep, he and Granger and Popson. All three of them are here."

I didn't quite know what to say. I really hadn't expected them to show up, I guess.

"I've asked another deputy to join me," Stephen said as he surveyed the crowded room.

"Good idea."

The presentation was scheduled to begin at 6:00 p.m., and Mom, ever punctual, got it rolling right on time. As she spoke, the crowd turned to face her at the front of the room, and Isaiah turned off a few of the lamps we'd placed around to light up the space with the help of a generator out back.

She walked through the history of the school. As she talked, architectural drawings of the school were on the screen, and she explained that most Rosenwald Schools were built using the same architectural plans. "So you can usually tell a Rosenwald building by looking for the large west-facing windows."

I could see several people nodding as they glanced at the big windows around them, but one head in particular caught my attention. Merle Popson was staring at the bottom- right corner of the far-right window, just where he'd slid that hose in to kill Charlotte and the children.

I didn't have much time to consider what it meant that he was so fixated on that spot, because just then, Isaiah said, "As you all know, thirteen people were killed here in 1954."

The room went quiet, and I saw Popson slowly turn his head back toward Isaiah. Something about his movement made me very nervous.

"For many years, our community has, at least publicly, acted like those murders did not happen."

From the corner of my eye, I saw Bud Granger start to rise to his feet with a finger raised, but Stephen laid a hand on his shoulder, and he sat back down.

"We aren't interested in holding a trial here. The days for that are long past." With a strength of spirit I didn't have, Isaiah looked Popson, Granger, and Tomlinson right in the eye. "We aren't looking for the courts to bring us justice here. They had their chance for that years ago, and that chance was not taken. So instead, we are hoping we can find a little truth here, a little reconciliation, maybe even a little transformation."

The murmur of the crowd was starting to grow, and I began to move toward the front of the room as we had planned. I saw Marcie and Nicole, hand in hand, come up the other side and felt Javier beside me. The night before, we'd discussed how it was less likely that people would get physical if teenagers were present. I also saw that the other deputy had slid into a corner at the back of the room.

Mom joined Isaiah at the podium as he continued. "As you'll see, we have chairs for all of you." Tyrice and his friends were unfolding chairs that had been tucked into the old coatroom. "If you would, please take a chair and help us create a large circle in the middle of the room. As you do, I'll explain what we're doing here."

I saw a few people slip out the door, but almost everyone stayed, including the three men we were most interested in. Slowly, a circle formed, and I saw Micah set his chair next to Tomlinson, and they briskly shook hands.

"This here is our talking stick." Isaiah held up a baby doll, and I recognized it as Henrietta's. She must have offered it for us to use, and I thought it a great tool. Who can be ugly with a tiny baby in your arms? "We will go around the circle, giving each person two minutes to speak without interruption. As long as you have this baby doll, you have the floor. After two minutes, I will cue the speaker to finish up and pass the baby doll to the next person."

I took my seat between Javier and Merle Popson. I had to work hard not to lean away from the older man.

Mom sat down and said, "Isaiah and I have prepared some questions, and we'd like to hear from anyone who wishes to share their thoughts in response to them. If you'd rather not share, just say 'Pass' when the doll reaches you. And if something someone else says in their minute is painful to you, just say 'Ouch,' and we'll pause and talk about that moment. Otherwise, though, your job here is mostly to listen. You'll get your turn to be heard, so you don't have to worry about jumping in or speaking your mind. You can just take the luxury of listening."

"Does everyone understand?" Isaiah asked.

Most of the heads in the circle nodded.

"Our first question," Isaiah said, "is what do you remember about this school?"

At first, I felt like Isaiah and Mom were throwing a soft pitch, taking it too easy on everyone, but as one person shared how they had gone to this school or their grandparents had and another said they'd driven past the school for years and never known what it was or had known it was there when they were in school but didn't think much about it, I could see how very quickly we were going deep into memory and personal attachments. I could also see very quickly that the racial divide over something as simple as a place was canyon-deep.

An older black man talked about how this place had been his biggest hope when he had "crazy dreams of being an engineer. Black boys didn't dream like that when I was young. But when I came into school, it seemed possible. Everything seemed possible."

When the baby came to Popson, he said, "Pass" in a sharp, quiet voice and moved the doll along. I wanted to be angry at that, to think it cowardly, but he looked stricken, a little pale. I could see a small twitch at the corner of his mouth. Something was happening in there.

I passed, as did Javier. We were here to listen, and we had agreed as a group that unless one of us really felt something we had to say would add to the circle, we would pass.

Kimberly, one of my classmates, shared how she came today because Blanch had invited her—and I saw him blush from his seat across the circle—and how she was glad she did because she hadn't realized that her friends' grandparents had gone to this school, that she hadn't realized segregation had been "alive and kickin'" for people she knew.

The baby slid into Tomlinson's hands, and I thought he would pass, too, but instead, he said, "Just knew it was a black school. I didn't know anyone who went here," his eyes glanced up to Micah, "not personally." He used one of the baby's legs to pass it over to Micah.

"This school was my safe place. I loved everything about it. The old stove, the rickety floorboards, even the secondhand textbooks that had all those white kids' names in them. I loved all of it, but I especially loved Miss Braxton."

I stole a glance over to Charlotte, who was watching from the corner, and saw her smile.

"But then, after," his eyes dropped to his shoes, "I couldn't really bear to be here anymore. I didn't want the building destroyed, so I kept an eye on it. But I didn't come in here. Not until a few weeks ago." He looked up at me.

The doll moved around the circle to Bud Granger, who also passed, and then back to Mom and then Isaiah, who shared how his dad had gone to a school like this one and how it had set him and his entire family on the path to higher education. "Education was the centerpiece of my family's life, all because of a little one-room school."

The air in the room felt heavy, but not suffocating. Just weighted with importance. Then, Isaiah asked the second question, "What do you remember about the murder of the schoolteacher Charlotte Braxton and twelve of her students?"

I took a deep breath and felt Javier's hand wrap around mine.

The first person to speak after two or three passed was a tiny black woman named Beulah. She couldn't have been more than five feet tall, and she sat curled into herself in the chair, her knee-highs rolled down around her ankles. "I was just out of high school then, working as a maid downtown. I didn't go to this school, went over the mountain, but I knew Charlotte."

I glanced over to my friend in the corner. She was leaning forward while she stroked a little boy's head that rested against her knee.

"We'd gone to dances and things together. She was a good person." She cast her eyes down to the wooden floor. "Don't know what kind of good that it did for her to die." She laid the baby doll in the lap of the man next to her.

A few people also shared about the school, about knowing the students, about Charlotte. One man said she was "tough, but I knew that meant she cared."

Then, the doll reached Popson, and he hesitated before he took it by the neck with three fingers. I thought for sure he'd pass, but instead, he perched that baby on his knee like it was alive and said quietly, "I didn't know that schoolteacher or any of them kids. I didn't know them at all."

He kept his eyes trained on the floor and took a deep breath, and again I thought he'd send the doll along. I kind of hoped he would.

"Back then, there wasn't much mixing." He looked up past everyone's head and to the back of the building by the wood stove. "Not like this." He kind of grimaced. "I guess we just didn't . . ."

I thought, for just a second, that he might confess. His faced had gone flush, and he made a sound in the back of his throat. But then he slid his hand under the baby doll's bum and passed her to me gently.

I tried to smile at him, look him in the eye, but he didn't look up. I held the baby in the crook of my arm and stared down at her. I didn't know whether to speak or not, but after a few seconds, I decided against it. Just then, I felt my pants move against my legs. Henrietta was sitting at my feet and smiling up at me.

A black man talked about how he remembered the murders, and he called them *murders*, about how he'd been here when they opened the building and found the bodies because he lived just up the road. "Still do," he said. He talked about seeing the death in their faces, the coldness, about how all that cold had sparked a blazing fire of hate in his soul. "It's

taken me forty years to work out that rage.
Forty years stolen from me. Forty years I gave
away."

I had been watching Henrietta to see
how she would take descriptions of her own
death, but she didn't seem bothered particularly. Maybe she's heard all this before, or
maybe Charlotte prepared the children for this
day. I suspected the latter.

When the doll reached Tomlinson, he
plunked it in his lap and looked at Isaiah. "I
know what you're doing here, bo—," he caught
himself, "man. I don't like it. It won't do anything but get people angry again. What good is
angry?" He held the doll out for Micah, who
took it gently.

Micah took a deep breath and let his
shoulders drop. He slid three, wide fingers
over the doll's skirt as she lay against his leg.
"Anger. Anger is natural. Normal. Healthy. It
tells us when something is wrong. But what
comes after anger, well, that's a choice. We can
decide to settle in with that wrongness and get
bitter." I felt his eyes land on his brother's face.
"Or we can swallow it and let it become sorrow. Or we can let it out, put it into the air,
and let it work to right that wrong. I'm tired of

this knot of anger in my belly. I'm tired of being so sad. So I'm letting the anger out today."

I felt the energy in the room charge up, the hairs on my arms stand on end. I felt Mom's eyes on my face and looked at her. She nodded and took Isaiah's hand. This was it.

"We know that Miss Braxton and those children—our friends," Micah looked around the room, "were murdered. And we know who murdered them."

His voice was solid and sure, but he wasn't making eye contact with anyone. Still, I could see a few heads around the room nodding. I didn't dare look at Popson, Tomlinson, or Granger.

"And while I want to believe that some kind of justice could be served by the courts, I don't believe it's the kind of justice we need." He laid the baby doll against his shoulder and rested his large hand against her back. I could just see her feet from where I sat, white and bare beneath his palm. "I think our justice needs to come in this place. Together." He looked first Granger, then Popson, then Tomlinson in the eye.

A lesser man would have made that statement sound like a threat, stirred up the crowd for a fight, a fight we wouldn't have been able to control. Darren's expression made me think that's what he'd been hoping for. But Micah's words had settled a weight on the room that was keeping everyone in their seats. We wouldn't have a fight today. We would have a decision.

Most people passed then, eager to hear what one of the white men who we all knew were guilty would say, and when the doll reached Granger, the room was so still I could hear the wood creak beneath us.

Bud Granger dropped the doll face down in his lap and looked Micah in the eye. "Let me tell you something, sir." His voice was laced with fire, and again, I braced myself for at least a verbal impact. But then, he took a breath and ran his fingers over his face.

"Let me tell you something. That day, that day, I don't know what we were doing. I've tried for years to remember, and I still don't know. We was mad, that's all. Just so mad. All I kept hearing was, 'That ni—'" he paused and glanced at Micah. "'That boy was out of line. He needs to be taught a lesson.'"

I stole a glance at Popson, then Tomlinson. They were both staring at their hands in their laps.

"I never did think it was right, what . . ." he lifted his head just a bit toward Popson, ". . . happened to that girl, but it wasn't our place to decide someone should be punished."

"Wasn't your place until—" I saw Darren start to rise, but Isaiah lifted a soft hand and Darren sat back down.

Granger sighed. "I know. It was all so confusing. All this talk of justice when one of our own was beaten up but nothing for that girl." He shook his head a tiny bit as if to clear it. "So that day, we'd been drinking down by the river. I guess between the alcohol and the three of us, well, we got ourselves an idea that we wouldn't let go."

The room was heavy with silence. I didn't dare move lest the spell of this moment break, but I tossed my eyes up to Mom and saw her looking right at Granger as if willing him to continue. Isaiah was staring at his clenched fists, and Darren looked like it was a sheer act of will to stay in his seat. But when I glanced at first Micah and then Charlotte, I saw tears on their cheeks and felt them well around my eyes.

"We didn't mean to hurt anybody. We really didn't." He looked up at Micah, his entire face a plea. "We didn't. We just thought it would make them sleep and then we'd go in and wreck some stuff. We didn't know it would ki—"

"That's enough." Someone spoke from the door of the school. "Bud, don't say another word." A tall, lean white man in a three-piece suit stood in the doorway. "Merle, Stu, Bud, let's go. You've said enough for today."

The three men glanced at each other, and I would have sworn they were just as surprised as the rest of us. They stood and walked to the door.

The man in the door walked over to Mom and handed her a card. "My name is Lester Ovar. I'm representing these men. Now, you'll do kindly to give me all the tapes of this conversation since they were obtained without my clients' permission." He put his hand out in front of Mom's face, palm up, like he expected her to pay him for his trouble.

"Sir, there are no tapes. This is just a conversation."

Ovar popped a breath into the air. "As if. Well, no matter, if those recordings should ever come to light, my clients will charge you with invasion of privacy, and you'll—and trust me on this—serve the full term."

Behind him, I could see Popson, Tomlinson, and Granger. They all looked slightly embarrassed, like their parents had shown up when they'd gotten in trouble at school, even though they were okay to take the punishment.

"None of you is to talk to any of my clients without my presence. Do you hear me?" His voice was lording, and he leaned forward a bit when he talked. He surveyed the entire circle.

I could have been imagining things, but it seemed like his eyes lingered longer on Micah's face.

Then he spun on one heel and followed his clients out the door.

The room grew still again, and everyone looked from face to face, searching for some explanation about what had happened. Finally, Isaiah spoke. "Well, friends, it seemed like maybe we were going to get to some truth here today," he took a deep breath, "and maybe we will again. But for now, maybe it's best if we all head on home, do some praying and some thinking."

It took a few minutes, but slowly, everyone filtered out. The guys and I put the tables back into the coatroom, and one by one the

people of Terra Linda went home in the dark
of the country night.

13.

When Mom, Isaiah, Javier, and I got to our house, I could feel the jagged reality of what had happened settle in my chest. We had almost heard a confession, and someone had stopped it. Actually, no, not someone, *something*. The weight of racism had let its momentum fall against that small gathering, and if we weren't careful, we'd all be crushed.

"Who do you think hired him?" Mom asked as she slid her feet under Isaiah's thigh on the sofa, a cup of chamomile tea in her hand.

"Who knows? The Citizen's Council? One of their wives, maybe?" He took a sip of his beer and leaned back. "I guess it doesn't really matter."

"Now what?" Javier said.

I wanted to rally and say something like, "Now, now we fight!" and lead us forth to battle like Nat Turner. But all I could see in my mind was Turner's bloody body hanging from a tree. What good is fighting when it gets you killed?

I took a deep breath and looked into the fire in front of me. Its warmth licked my skin, and I could feel my own resolve shriveling in its flames. I heard the door open behind me. "So I have some news . . ." Marcie was standing right behind me.

I turned to look at her over my right shoulder. Her light-brown skin was pink from the cold air outside.

"There's evidence we don't know about."

She sat down on the arm of the sofa next to Mom. "My great-uncle Hubert . . . you've met him, Mary . . . well, he was at the gathering today. Tall, skinny man. Black hat."

I nodded.

"He caught up to me at home and gave me a photograph. He said someone—he didn't say who—had given it to him this afternoon, that they'd slipped it into his hand as he was leaving."

She handed the photo to Mom. Mom's head pulled back on her neck, and then she passed the photo to Isaiah, who scowled at the image for a long time before sending it on. I was fairly sure I wouldn't have a fingernail left by the time it got to me, and when it did, I let out a puff of air. "Am I seeing what I think I'm seeing?"

Isaiah stood up and started pacing behind the couch. "I think so. Didn't someone tell us Granger drove a '49 Olds? And that's definitely the school."

"And that's definitely a hose running from the car to the window."

Someone had taken a photograph of the murders.

I stared at the picture and felt the living room recede behind me. I could feel the breeze of fall move the hair at my ears, and I could smell leaves in the air. I heard the car's engine running and the laughter of the three boys in front of me. It felt so real.

Marcie grabbed my elbow and leaned around to look into my face. "You okay?"

I gave my shoulders a shudder and nodded.

"No, really? Don't give me that shrugging crap."

I looked up into my best friend's face and saw her brown eyes looking straight into me. "Yeah, really. I'm not awesome. But I'm okay."

She dropped her arm around my shoulder and stared at the picture with me.

We sat for a long time that night trying to decide what to do. Javier wanted to take the picture to the police, to Stephen specifically, but Marcie wasn't sure that was the right thing, and I wasn't either. I was surprised by my feelings. This morning I had been hoping for a fight, and now, *now*, I thought we needed to take it slow. *And* we needed to talk with Micah and most definitely with Charlotte.

Mom took the photo and made two copies for each of us and told us to put them in separate places, just in case. Then she gave Marcie the original. "Make sure Hubert gets this back, and thank him for us. Maybe suggest he pass it back to the person who gave it to them. They shared it for a reason, but it's still their property."

Marcie nodded and headed for the door. We all needed to sleep on this . . . as if sleep was going to be restful tonight.

The next morning, Mom, Isaiah, and I headed over to Shady Run. A quick text to everyone had settled the arrangements late the night before. We needed to talk, and we needed Charlotte there, too. Mom had called the high school to let them know I'd be late.

I wasn't feeling particularly good. A bad night's sleep plus a lot of stress made me irritable and gave me one of those headaches that isn't bad enough to need ibuprofen but that still settles against the back of my forehead and drums. Plus, if I was honest, I was overwhelmed by all that was happening. It was one thing to try to save a school and solve a murder in the abstract. It was another to be brought into the midst of a legal battle and have to sit with murderers and the ghosts of the murdered in the same room.

As everyone pulled out chairs and set out the donuts and coffee that Mom had known would be necessary, I went and sat on the floor at the side of Charlotte's chair while she fixed Henrietta's braids. The teacher was just a couple of years older than me, but she had the presence of someone who understands life and frail moments better than anyone I'd known. I suppose fifty years as a ghost who tended children would do that for you.

When she was done with Henrietta's hair, she laid a soft hand on my shoulder while I stared at the chalkboard. I reached up and placed my hand over hers. "We don't know what to do, Charlotte. I don't know what to do."

"You don't have to, Mary. This is not your burden to carry on your own. Just because you were the one brought here to find us doesn't mean this is your responsibility. Don't take on more than you can handle." She turned me toward her gently. "And don't think you're more important than you are." She smiled. "You're just one of many here, and we don't need a savior. We need a friend."

You know how sometimes people say something that cuts right to the quick of your struggle, how it flays open your own burdens *and* your presumptions and spreads them wide for you to see? Here I was thinking that somehow I had to make this decision, that because I was the person who had first seen Charlotte and the children my opinion was most important. It wasn't. It was, in so many ways, least important . . . but my nature, the way Mom had taught me to be responsible, and some white privilege—which I wouldn't really be able to lay words against until I was much older—were all operating in that moment to make me think that somehow I had to be the one to make a decision and bring it about.

I leaned my head against Charlotte's knee and took a deep breath. Even decades later, I could still smell the lavender of her clothes. Then, I sat back, pushed myself to standing, and took her hand as she stood beside me.

For the next three hours, we talked and shouted—Micah, Shamila, Mr. Meade (he'd called in a substitute for the day), Isaiah, Mom, Marcie, Nicole, Javier, me, Charlotte, and Darren. We swam from questions about calling Stephen to talking to Hubert to showing the photo to Granger, Tomlinson, and Popson ourselves.

"Listen." Charlotte's one word brought all our righteous fidgeting to a halt. She looked each of us in the eye. "We are going to listen." Leaning in close and speaking in that quiet voice that carries for miles and seems to be the special talent of skilled teachers, she said, "The police failed us once before. I know why. I understand the times in which I lived. I hold no grudge, but I also hold no confidence in them."

Now that I could understand. Apart from Stephen, I didn't hold much hope for the police department either, not after they ignored the murder of children, not after all the murders of black people I'd seen on the news.

"But it's more than that," Charlotte continued. "The thing is the children and I don't need justice. What we need is to understand."

"What's there to understand?" Micah began but Charlotte silenced him with a gently-raised hand.

"We know that they were racist. We know that they were mad at you, Micah. We know that they were teenage boys who'd probably had too much to drink. We know all of that." She looked at the children around the room—some drawing on the chalkboard, tiny sketches that we could never see, and some were playing jacks in the corner. "We need to understand what their hearts look like now. We need to see if they are sorry, and if they are, we need to understand why. Are they sorry they got caught? Or are they really sorry that they killed us?"

I looked at Charlotte's face and saw tears pooling in her eyes.

"Justice will do us no good; we are dead. But I don't think it'll do you all any good at this point, either. We know the truth, and unless these men are cold-blooded killers without feelings, we also know that they have walked around for fifty years with the weight of what they've done. I, for one, think that's justice enough for one lifetime."

I felt something in my chest turn over into the light. I hadn't been seeking justice. Justice is about punishment with the hope of redemption. Nope, I had been seeking revenge, and revenge shadows a soul something awful—just look at Popson, Granger, and Tomlinson.

Charlotte leaned back in her chair. "What we need is understanding. We need to see that these men feel remorse. I need to see this. Yesterday, I saw three men who were broken—they carry the weight of the day we died in their bones, in the wrinkles on their faces. I need to know what is breaking them," she sighed.

"You need to hear that so you can forgive them," Isaiah said quietly.

"No, son. I have already forgiven them. We all have." The children had gathered behind her now, knowing as only people who have lived together for decades can, that she needed them. "This isn't about forgiveness. This is about freedom. Until we shine light into this, we cannot go home."

Henrietta slid over to me and sat on my lap. "I want to go home, Mary. I really want to go home."

I slid my arms around her and let my head drop against hers on my shoulder. "Okay, Henrietta. Okay, we'll get you home."

It was a hard conversation that showed, again, the ways our society's racial attitudes shaped our perspectives. I moved through defensiveness to justification to despair as we talked, but at the end, when we came to our decision, I felt settled, assured, together with these kind, flawed, brave people in this struggle.

We made the choice to blow up the photo hanging both at the school and around town. At the same time, we would invite Granger, Popson, and Tomlinson back to Shady Run, with their lawyer if they'd like. It was time this was all brought to light, but we didn't think we needed court action. Charlotte didn't want that.

It wasn't easy to get to a place where we agreed with her, though. Many of us—Mom, Isaiah, Darren—wanted to hand the photo over to Stephen Douglass and prepare for a trial. "Justice needs to be served," Darren said several times.

"I agree," Mom said. "It could be dangerous for us to take this on. There's no guarantee that those men will hear us, let along talk to us. And if they talk, what are we going to do?"

So the blown-up pictures went up all over Terra Linda and Lexington. Marcie had asked Hubert to ask the person who had given him the image if that was okay, and they had agreed. Soon, the library, most of the storefronts on Main Street, the local black churches and some of the white ones, too, had this image hanging there. We didn't add any commentary. We didn't give context. We just hung the pictures and trusted that putting the light on this moment would do the trick.

A week after the pictures went up, our lawyer called Popson, Granger, and Tomlinson's lawyer and explained what we were seeking. Then, Micah, acting on behalf of the Shady

Run Rosenwald School Association, an organization that he was founding with some other alumni, invited the men to the school on Sunday afternoon under the following conditions: Lawyers were welcome; police officers were not. The three men could bring their spouses if they wished but no one else, and we would not publicize the meeting or tell anyone but the original group of us about it. We would record the conversation but we agreed—and would sign a document to that fact—that we would not share the recording with anyone unless all parties present signed a form granting permission.

Almost immediately, we heard from Granger and Tomlinson. They would be there with their lawyer. We took hope in that. But then, on Wednesday, Popson wrote to say he wouldn't be coming. "No" was all the note scrawled on the bottom of our letter said.

I was disappointed, but not surprised. Still, I knew we'd only get the insight we needed to get Henrietta home if we had all three men there.

Mom and I decided to head over to the Popson house on Thursday afternoon. We thought a personal invitation might do the trick. Maybe he just needed a little persuasion. Maybe if we showed kindness he would come.

We parked our car on the street in front of the Popson's tidy ranch house on the hill by the high school. Their boxwoods were cut into neat hedges, and the maple out front was circled by a perfectly symmetrical bed of orange mulch. I walked beside Mom up the concrete path and stood at her side as she rang the bell.

An older woman in an apron opened the door and smiled. "Yes? Can I help you?"

"Mrs. Popson?" Mom asked.

"Yes, that's me."

"My name is Elaine Steele and this is my daughter Mary." At the sound of our names, Mrs. Popson went from Mrs. Clause to bride of Chucky. Her jaw hardened, and from behind the door, she brought her hand, which was wrapped around a flour-covered wooden spoon.

"Get off my property. Now." That spoon came forward as she reached for the handle on the storm door that was between us. "Now."

I looked at Mom, but she didn't move.

"Mrs. Popson, we are only here to invite your husband . . ."

"I told that lawyer you were going to start harassing us, and here you are."

I took a deep breath, squared my hips and said the first thing that came to mind. "Charlotte Braxton is a friend of mine."

This stopped Mrs. Popson short. "Who?!"

"Charlotte Braxton. The teacher in that school. She's my friend. And so are the kids there, especially Henrietta. She likes to sit on my lap."

Whether she thought I was insane or had just gotten very confused, I can't say, but she grew very still.

I took this as my opportunity to speak. "I know those people, ma'am. I know Charlotte loves the scent of lavender and that Henrietta loves to have people rub her back. I know the boys shoot marbles with the best of them and that one tiny little guy, TJ, really, really loves macaroni and cheese. They're my friends, see?"

Now, Mrs. Popson's brow began to drop. "Those people are dead, girl. They can't be your friends."

"Oh, but they are. I can see—"

Mom's hand laid gently against my arm, and Mrs. Popson's eyes followed it. "We care about those people," Mom spoke softly but clearly. "We know about their families and what they wore to school each day. As Mary said, we even know what they liked to eat. They are friends to us."

Mrs. Popson leaned back a little. I could see the spoon down by her waist, but she wasn't brandishing it anymore. It was just hanging there, limp and sprinkling white power on her doorstep.

"We aren't trying to stir up trouble. We aren't even trying to get anyone in trouble. We just want to know the truth so that we can all have some peace. ALL of us." Mom leaned toward the door when she said that last sentence.

I felt something shift then, a tiny giving to of the way that everyone in Terra Linda had chosen. A small tear in the shroud of lies and apathy. I held my breath.

"I'll tell him to go."

The older woman's voice was so quiet I almost didn't hear her. But Mom did. "Thank you, Mrs. Popson," Mom said. "We hope you'll come, too. Maybe bring some of those cookies that smell so good." There it was again, Mom's way of drawing someone close with what they loved. "I'm going to make brownies, and Mary here whips up a mean batch of Rice Krispies treats."

A soft nod. Then, just as she closed the door, she met our eyes, and I could see the

long, narrow tunnel that was fifty years of
grief.

14.

When Sunday arrived, my stomach felt like a twisted-up dish rag. I couldn't even eat breakfast because I was so nervous. I'd spent the night imagining fists and burning bottles. But Mom made me choke down some maple oatmeal, and I felt a little better—much to my chagrin—after I ate it. Sometimes, it would be really nice if she didn't know best.

Marcie, Nicole, Tyrice, and Micah were already at Shady Run when we arrived. They'd opened up the building and were painting the coatroom. We'd all agreed that we wanted the school to look as nice as it could, but I also knew they needed to keep busy. People don't paint at 9:00 a.m. on a Sunday because it's fun.

The students were in their desks listening as Charlotte give them a lesson in manners. "Now, we know people won't be able to greet us, but that doesn't mean that we need to be rude to them. We will smile politely and stay out of the way, won't we?" Twelve tiny heads nodded.

I could see that Charlotte had gotten the children as cleaned up as they could be. Well, really, I couldn't see that. No matter what they did to their physical bodies or clothes, they always looked the same. But from the way the boys moved, I could tell they'd spiffed up their clothes—no sitting on the floor, no running around and bumping into the chalk boards. And Henrietta kept touching the braids at her neck as if they were precious. I found myself mirroring her as I checked to be sure that the French braid Mom had done for me was holding steady.

Today was a big deal. I was only beginning to understand how big.

The invitation had said 2:00 p.m. Enough time for everyone to go to church—we figured we needed all the prayers we could get—grab lunch at the Caboose Diner, and head on over to the school.

Isaiah arrived next with a huge sheet cake, and Shamila came soon after with two trays one of fruit and one of veggies. Mom and I had already laid our cookies and Rice Krispies treats (Mom insisted I keep my word and make them, and it seemed useless to point out that I wasn't the one who had promised them.) Mr. Meade brought gallons of iced tea, and Javier arrived with three big bags of potato chips. We were all set.

Our plan had been to settle in and talk over how things would go for a while, strategize what we'd do or say if the men confessed. How would we honor their confession, hear it, recognize it for what it was, but not resort to anger?

We'd just settled into our circle of chairs to prepare when the door opened. An older black couple walked in slowly. They were studying every part of the building, their gazes moving from window to desk to chalkboard. I don't know how I could tell, but I knew they recognized this space, had been here before.

Isaiah looked at Micah, then stood and walked over with an outstretched hand. "My name is Isaiah Johnson. Welcome to the Shady Run School. How can I help you?"

The man spoke. "My name is Ned Jones, and this here is my wife, Roberta. Our daughter Henrietta went to this school."

My eyes ran to Henrietta, who was standing by the chalkboard with her hands slack at her sides and her mouth open a sliver. Charlotte moved quickly behind her and put two hands on the girl's shoulders.

Mom stood and walked to the couple with a hand extended. "Mr. and Mrs. Jones, I'm Elaine Steele. It's nice to meet you. Would you like to have a seat?" She angled her body toward the circle of chairs, and Javier moved over a seat to open up the two just in front of them.

"We didn't mean to interrupt a meeting," Mr. Jones said, and I couldn't tell if he was apologetic or annoyed. "We heard about what's been happening here from friends— we live up in Charlottesville now—and came the first day we could to see what we could see."

"Yes, sir," Isaiah said, standing to greet the couple as well. "We're glad you're here, and I expect Micah, er, Mr. Tindall would be happy to explain what we've been doing here."

At the sound of Micah's name, Mrs. Jones looked up sharply. "Micah Tindall. You're the boy who caused all this trouble." She took two steps forward and raised her cane. "You couldn't leave well-enough alone, and our daughter—our *only* daughter—is dead."

Micah had stood and begun to walk over, but Mrs. Jones' words stopped him cold. He dropped his head.

Out of the corner of my eye, I saw movement. Henrietta rushed by me and stood bolt-upright in front of her mom and dad. "No, no. Mr. Tindall is nice. He's been here to visit us all these years, and you've never come, not even once." The little body began to shake with sobs.

I stepped over to stand beside Mom. "Mr. and Mrs. Jones, my name is Mary Steele. I know you're angry, and you have every right to be. But maybe it's not Micah you need to be mad at . . ."

Mr. Jones took a step toward me and said, "Ms. Steele, I know you mean well, but I suggest you mind your own business."

Mom's hand wrapped around mine, and I took a deep breath.

Then, Charlotte was behind me. "Tell them that Henrietta was a great student, that she had perfect penmanship and always won the good citizenship award."

I looked down at the little girl in front of me. "I know that Henrietta did well in school here, that she wrote right pretty and was kind to everyone. She won a Citizenship Award, didn't she?"

The old woman looked into my face, and I could see her lip quiver for just a second. "Yes, yes, she did. Got an award for being 'Teacher's Best Helper,' too."

"Told her she needed to be careful about brown-nosing. Some people didn't like that," Henrietta's dad said, his gaze now out the window.

"I did like it," Charlotte said quietly.

"I expect, sir, that Charlotte—Miss Braxton, liked having Henrietta's help. I think she probably liked Henrietta very much."

"Mr. and Mrs. Jones, won't you please sit down with us?" Mom said. "We'd like a chance to explain what we are doing here, about how Mr. Tindall has brought us together to try to make some things—the things we can—right."

Mrs. Jones took a deep breath and then made her way to one of the chairs, her husband behind her.

I realized, just then, that we had made a big mistake in our work here. We had assumed that we'd involved everyone in town who had been hurt by these murders. We'd even invited the murderers into the building, but we'd made no specific effort to contact the families, the parents, and brothers and sisters of these students. I gasped. I had to bite my lower lip to keep from crying. What had we been doing?

I wanted to pretend that it was somehow the family's fault that they didn't know, to act like we'd done everything we could do, but of course, we hadn't. We'd focused on how this affected us here in Terra Linda now—and that wasn't wrong—but we'd forgotten that thirteen families had suffered then and that we needed to repair those relationships, too, to give our apologies and our words for them, too.

I looked around at my friends, at Mom, and from the way they kept their eyes to the floor I figured they were having the same moment of realization, too. I think we were all trying to figure out what the best thing to do now was.

Darren was the one who spoke first. "Mr. and Mrs. Jones, I'm Darren Tindall, Micah's brother. I used to ride my bike by your house every evening on the way home from football practice, and you, Mrs. Jones, would wave as you swept the front porch. You were kind folks, and I'm so sorry for what happened to you."

Mr. Jones gave a crisp nod of the head.

"I'm sorry, too," Isaiah joined. "We should have contacted you right away when we started all of this. I can't rightly tell you why we didn't." He looked around at all of us. "But I'm sorry. We all are."

Every head in that circle nodded.

Mrs. Jones took a deep, shuddering breath. "Never mind that," she said in a quiet but solid voice after a few minutes. "What's going on here now?"

"How can we help?" Mr. Jones said with a gaze fixed on Micah.

It's amazing to me what an apology—sincere and brave—can do. Sometimes it felt likes miracles rode in on whispers.

Isaiah began to explain what we'd planned for the afternoon, and the Jones' leaned in to listen while Henrietta leaned against her mother's leg and cried.

After a few minutes, Mr. Jones said, "Well, I reckon I best go be sure the rest of the parents' know about it. Most of us moved away—too hard to see this place and these people." I could almost feel his gaze trying to resist a glance at Micah. "But we're mostly close. What time did you say this gathering starts?"

"Two o'clock. Please extend our apologies for not contacting them sooner. Here, you can use my phone," Isaiah said.

"Thank you, but I've got my own." Mr. Jones took the biggest smartphone I've ever seen off his belt and headed for the door. When he saw my expression, he said, "I have Snapchat, too," and walked out the door.

Within three hours, the room was full of people, mostly the parents of the children who had died, but a few of the folks from our healing circle the other day were there, too, former students and community members, and I was suddenly very aware that what we had promised Popson, Granger, and Tomlinson—a quiet, intimate space to share—was gone. I didn't think they'd be too thrilled about that.

Mom and Isaiah must have had the same thought because they were down the road a ways so that they could explain to the men what had happened since we last spoke. Seemed wise to me. Better to have the men lose it out there than in here, where people were already pretty stirred up. I'd had two conversations with two mothers already—Terrence's and Davy's moms—that made me nervous that things could get ugly, no matter what we did. It's not a quiet, peaceful space when a seventy-five-year-old woman tells you that she's going to stab her cane through the throats of the men who did this.

Things had gotten out of hand. Very out of hand.

Mr. Meade had decided to go ahead and ask Stephen Douglas to come down and bring a deputy or two with him, and I was glad they came and that they came in plain clothes. I felt better with them there. As much as the police were partially to blame for this horrible, horrible situation, I still was a white girl who had grown up to trust police officers. Marcie, well, not so much.

She liked Stephen well enough, but she'd once told me a story about how her grandmother sat her down and said, "Now, when you see a police car, you walk slowly in the other direction. You don't run. You don't look nervous, but you go the other way." Hence, while I was glad the deputies came in plain clothes, we didn't need people feeling even more nervous than they already were.

At 2:00 p.m., I looked out the window to see Mom and Isaiah talking with all three men by the side of the road. Mrs. Popson was there with two other women, Granger and Tomlin-son's wives, I imagined. From the way the men were standing with their feet wide apart and Mom's attempts to lay a hand on an arm now and then, I figured things weren't going well. But we had people here, now, who needed to talk, so I caught Micah's eye. He nodded and began encouraging people to take a seat. I sat with my back to the door because no one else was and waited for everyone to settle.

I could feel my heart in my ears, and I thought for sure I would need to hydrate soon since I was pouring out half my body's water through my palms. I had no idea what I was going to say, but I knew something needed to be said—and for reasons I still don't under-stand, I knew I had to be the one to say it.

When everyone was settled in a chair, I began. "My name is Mary Steele. I know most of you don't know who I am, and there's no reason you should. I just grew up here in Terra Linda . . . like many of you did, I imagine." I saw heads nodding. "I'm here in this school to-day because I care about it. I care about its his-tory—both the good, amazing, fun things that happened here and the horrible ones."

"Mm-hmm," someone said from across the circle.

"I'm also here because my friends care about this place. Many of you know Micah and Darren Tindall, the two men who have kept the schoolhouse standing for over fifty years." People nodded in their direction. "You may know Mr. Tom Meade, the high school history teacher, and Shamila Meadows from the historical society. And these are my friends Javier, Marcie, and Nicole. We all care about this place and the people who love it."

I took my time, even though I wanted to flip my chair over and bolt out the door. I looked each person in the eye because Mom had taught me that eye contact establishes connection, and I knew I needed them to see me for real in order to say what I needed to say next.

"I know some of the people you love, too. Charlotte Braxton. Henrietta Jones. DaShawn Baker. Terrence Lucian. Daisy Bates. Davy Edwards. Lucy Montrose. Beatrice Norman. Joan Calvin. Brenda Taliaferro. Michael Davis. TJ Madison. Belle Drew." I looked at each child standing around Charlotte in the corner as I said their names. They smiled and waved. I tried to keep my composure. I didn't need to look crazy as well as sound it.

"What you mean you know them?" a woman with full cheeks and long eyelashes asked. "You studied them?"

"Well, yes, I have done some research to learn about them. I know their birthdays, and I knew most of your names before you came. But I also know their favorite colors and what foods they hate." I looked up at Charlotte, and she nodded. She glanced at Henrietta and then sent her over to me. "I know them. I can see them. They are still here."

I took a breath and then Henrietta's hand.

I knew the minute they could see her because, of course, someone gasped, and another person said, "No!" I didn't see those people though. I was looking at Mr. and Mrs. Jones . . . it was something like watching a partner watch his love come down the aisle at a wedding. You know the full extent of his adoration from the look on his face. It was no different here.

Mrs. Jones sat very still for a moment, and then she reached out her arms wide. Henrietta didn't wait even one second. She was in that embrace faster than I could exhale. Her dad, well, he took a minute longer. First he looked at me, then at her, then at me again.

When I nodded, he knelt down and shoved his face next to hers.

It was a beautiful moment, but I didn't get to watch it long. Suddenly, the room was full of questions, shouted questions, and I felt the energy ramping to a cliff that we were all going to fall off of. A panic started to rise in my chest as people stood and moved toward me.

But then, a long shadow stepped in front of me, and I looked up to see the back of Micah's head. "We know you've got a lot of questions, folks. We know. But if you'll kindly sit back down, we will try our best to answer all of them." His voice boomed like a whisper through the room, and all the frenzy settled. People began to sit back down, and I took a breath I didn't know I had been refusing.

I saw Mom and Isaiah slip into two chairs they'd pulled into the circle next to me, and I caught Mom's eye. A slight shake of the head, and I knew we'd lost them . . . maybe for good.

I didn't have much time to think about that though, because the questions were rising again. I imagined an ocean stirring up in a storm . . . if I didn't sail quickly, the white caps were going to swamp me. I took the doll that

Micah held out to me, and I began to tell my story, of ghosts and cemeteries, of not knowing, of last year. I talked quietly. I just didn't have it in me to yell any of this.

As I spoke, I felt Charlotte come up behind me, and when I told about the morning I'd appeared here in the school, she laid an arm on my shoulder. I paused as people gasped, but this time, everyone stayed quiet. I explained the final bit of what was mine to tell, about Micah coming in and finding me, about how this all started, and then I grew silent.

Charlotte motioned for the rest of the children to join us in the circle, and as they slid carefully between the people seated in that circle, I watched them walk over to me so I could hug them—and reveal them—to everyone.

The next hour was made up of tears—both joyful as parents saw children for the first time in fifty years—and sorrowful,l since some of the parents hadn't made it. DaShawn Baker cried out with pain when Micah told him that his parents had died just the year before.

There was nothing easy, though, even in the joy, because now, now Darren's anger looked like a summer rain compared to the maelstrom that was the parents' rage. They shouted at Isaiah, Micah, Mom, and especially me—and who could blame them—about why we hadn't called them right away. I had no answer except to say, "I'm sorry." I would carry that question for decades.

They wanted to know why their children were still here, why they hadn't been able to go in peace, and they wanted the answer from me. No matter how many times I said, "I don't know" or explained that I didn't even know why I could see their children let alone why they were there, it didn't help. And as frustrated and exhausted as I was, I didn't blame them. I would want answers from me, too.

Eventually, Mom, Mr. Meade, Shamila, and Isaiah were able to get people seated, their children at their feet or in their laps, so we could talk more. Charlotte gathered the rest of the children between her and I as she joined the circle. We had important questions to discuss, and now, now the stakes were even higher for how we'd answer them.

15.

Our gathering at the school went late into the evening, and by the time we were done, everyone was exhausted, even the children and Charlotte, who—until then—I hadn't thought capable of getting tired. But I suppose that much emotional pain and anger and joy can drain even the dead.

We did make some decisions, though. Hard-fought choices about how to proceed. Some of the parents thought we should tear the school down, destroy the place where murders occurred. Charlotte and I were quick to point out, though, that this did nothing for what she called "the ghost problem." That got a chuckle. As she said, even without the building, it was likely that she and the children would still be bound to this location, only this time they'd be without shelter, which may seem incidental when thinking of ghosts but would, altogether, make their days pretty brutal, especially in the winter. They couldn't feel things, but they could remember cold. No, that wasn't an option.

This wasn't the first time I wished I'd read up on how ghosts work, by the way. Ever since I'd met Moses, I'd thought about doing an epic trip to the library and reading my way through a weekend's worth of paranormal investigations and scientific studies. Each time I'd started to do that, though, I'd decided against it. The "how" of ghosts and even more the mechanism that made me see them seemed relatively unimportant overall. After all, no amount of knowing made it possible for me to change anything.

What we could change, however, was what the living humans did, and that's where we got into some heated, well, let's call them discussions. A few of the parents suggested we create a memorial to Charlotte and the twelve children in the building, and as far as I could tell, everyone thought that was a great idea.

Okay, maybe Charlotte didn't love it, but I suspect that was more about her aspersion of all photos of herself rather than a moral objection.

The differences of opinion arose when someone said the entire building should become a shrine, that we have it consecrated and turn it into a chapel. Very quickly, the religious differences in the group arose. The Baptists wanted it to be an active congregation, and the Catholics wanted a quiet place of prayer. Some of the parents didn't want any such thing, since they weren't religious, and others just thought that a waste of a perfectly good space. It was Charlotte that settled this one.

"Parents, please." She silenced the room with a quiet voice and a raised hand. "I understand what you are wanting here. You want a place where your children will be remembered."

"And you, too," a father piped up in the back of the room. Charlotte silenced him with a stare.

"But this has never been a place of worship, and I assure you that neither your children nor I are saints." This brought a few snickers. "What if we did what Micah Tindall has wanted all along? What if we created a community center where people can come and

learn and celebrate and even hold church meetings if they need the space for that." She surveyed the room. "That way, everyone in the
community can use the building, and everyone
can have a space to come to terms with the
things that have happened here."

A mom a few seats over from me asked,
"When you say community, you mean black
community, right?"

I glanced around and saw a lot of heads
nodding.

"No." Charlotte said the one syllable
with the force of a sledgehammer. "The whole
community."

The grumbling was beginning quickly
this time.

"Please, listen." Charlotte used that word
so well. "It was separating people that got us
into this horrible situation in the first place,
and while I'd hope that in the last fifty years
that I'd been sitting in this schoolhouse things
had changed, it sounds—from what my friends
tell me," she looked at me and then at Darren,
"things aren't that much different. Is it right
that still on Sundays black folks and white
folks go to different churches? And that you
all probably don't have many white friends?"

The silence was brief but deep. Then, a man across from me said, "But Miss Charlotte, that's not our choice—"

Charlotte cut him off mid-sentence. "I know. I know that we have never set up the laws or the rules about who knows who. I know. But listen to us here, we are acting like those laws and rules is, excuse me, ARE right."

"But we want a safe space, a place where we can be ourselves." This time, the speaker was Mrs. Jones.

Isaiah leaned into the circle. "What if we could assure you that this space would be safe, even if white people were invited in?"

"How you going to do that, son?" Daisy's father said.

"I don't know yet." He leaned back. "But if I know this group, I know we can do anything we set our minds to."

So that was it. We would keep going with our original plan to create a community center, but now it would be a space for all people of the community— black, white, brown, everyone. Javier had noted that his church was always looking for places to hold after-school tutoring sessions where people could gather together. For the most part, it looked like people left satisfied, or at least not angry.

None of us, though, mentioned what we'd intended to do here today. Popson, Granger, and Tomlinson never came up. Somehow, we all agreed without a word that this new plan was too fragile, these parents too charged with grief and joy and all the mix of that which must come when you find out your child is a ghost.

The burden of waiting for that conversation felt very, very heavy as I lay down to sleep that night. I've never been good with waiting. I like to get things over with and deal with the consequences if they come.

Today, though, we had carried the consequences to, maybe, a bit of healing. Maybe. But my dreams, my dreams weren't hopeful that night.

The next morning came very early, and before I knew it, I could hear Javier's characteristic three beeps from the driveway. I was still in bed. It was going to be a long day.

How I managed to be out the door in less than five minutes, I couldn't say, except to praise the glory of pigtails. As I raced out the door, I blew Mom a kiss and dove in Javier's front seat, almost breaking my neck in the process as the weight of my body collided with the force of my turned head when I noticed people in the back seat. Marcie and Nicole were there, all grins.

I glanced at Javier, and his grin was the biggest of them all. *Uh-oh. What do these three have planned?*

"Do I have to wear a blindfold this time?" I said to Javier.

"A blindfold? What?! No, wait, I don't want to know." Marcie shared from behind Javier.

I shot her a pointed glance. "So what's happening?"

Javier backed out of the driveway. "You'll see."

We drove down the hill and out through town, past the locks on the river and over into Lexington. By now, I was sure we were going to miss school, but I was so intrigued I didn't care. Okay, I almost didn't care.

Javier skirted the car down Main Street, and Nicole made us promise to stop at the Gelateria later that afternoon.

"Wait. We're going to be here all day?"

If a smile could break a face, Javier's would have cracked in half.

When the car turned into the brick-fronted parking garage, I had a sense of where we might be going, but I was still unsure why. We parked and made our way back down to the street and through a pair of glass doors into the County Clerk's office.

Now, during the last two years of my life, I had done enough research to know that this was where all the public records of the county lived. Ah, this was a research trip.

A normal teenager might have been annoyed to find that her friends had broken her out of school for the day only to take her to do research in old papers, but not me. I was thrilled. Talk about face-breaking smiles.

As we passed by a high countertop, Javier waved to a dark-haired young woman in the corner, and she pointed to a table in the back, where I saw ten or twelve *huge* books stacked. Oh, it was going to be a good day.

I gave Javier a quick peck on the check, and he whispered, "You needed some time to rest, to think. So, here you go."

Talk about a man who gets me.

I dropped my backpack by my chair and heard my metal water bottle clang through the room. I'm certain I turned fourteen shades of red as I glanced to see if anyone was looking. But since we were the only people here besides the staff, I was spared that embarrassment.

I glanced at my watch—8:30 a.m. I had hours of looking through papers ahead, and I began bouncing in my seat. "What did your friend get down for us, Javi?"

"I asked her to gather any documents that related to the school or to the children who went there. So I suspect these are birth records, maybe death records, too. Marriage certificates, maybe court cases. I don't know really. You're the historian, after all."

I blushed again. Man, this guy knew how to get to my heart. I slid my hand onto his knee under the table and saw the color hit his cheeks. Too cute.

It didn't take me long to disappear into the stories. In the first book I picked up, I found the birth records for Beatrice Norman and Terrence Lucian. I jotted down dates and parents' names and then paused to imagine how the Lucians had looked on this August day in 1947. Their faces smooth and joyful.

I went digging next for the Normans' and Lucians' marriage certificates and quickly found both, which listed their parents' names. I was on the trail of family trees, and I wasn't to be stopped. I don't really know what I thought I'd find there, what I hoped all this information would give me, give us. But if you've ever done genealogical work, you know that the purpose doesn't matter; the stories are always going to find you if you keep looking.

Two hours later, I looked up and saw that Marcie and Nicole had left, and Javier was sleeping in the chair next to me. I smiled and went back in.

Mostly, I found more of the same—birth dates, parents' names, marriage certificates—and within a few hours, I had compiled three or four generations of family history for a few of the kids. I couldn't go back much further from there, though, because of slavery. Those records would be in plantation books, for the most part, since it was likely that these kids' great-great grandparents, maybe even their great-grandparents were slaves somewhere nearby. But that was research for another day.

A quick peek at my watch told me it was 2:00 p.m. Nicole and Marcie had dropped by a couple hours earlier to suggest we meet at the Gelateria at 3:00 o'clock, and I'd agreed. Even I can only take so much old handwriting. But I wanted to do one last bit of research before I quit.

I grabbed the marriage index again and looked up "Merle Popson." Yep, there he was marrying Susan Best on March 23, 1955, just six months after the school fire. I peeled back through the years to find his parents' records and her parents' and on and on into the 1840s. Slavery wasn't a wall for white folks' genealogy, after all.

Then, I went over to the computers— with a smile at Javier—and pulled up the census records online. Shamila had taught me how to do all this last year, and I had quickly become a regular visitor to the online genealogy sites, playing around to put together Javier's, Marcie's, Nicole's, and my mom's genealogies. Today, though, I had something else in mind.

I opened the 1850 census and typed in "Obadiah Popson," the name of Merle Popson's great-great-grandfather. There he was, living in the Poplar District, the same area where the Shady Run School would eventually be built. Next, I went into the slave schedules and searched his name again. And there, I saw what I had been looking for—in 1850, Obadiah Popson owned twenty-three slaves: five men, seven women, and eleven children.

I wasn't sure what I was going to do with that information. I wasn't going to threaten or use it as a sword, but something in me—maybe the same force that carried me to the school in the first place—told me that I would need to know this sometime soon.

Javier tapped me on the shoulder, and I stared up at him. Time for gelato.

I've always been one of those people who can totally lose track of today when I'm working on something for tomorrow or from yesterday. That phrase "being present" is one I should probably tattoo on the back of my hand.

But the thing is I am present, very much present when I'm doing this work. I drop myself whole into whatever I'm researching and begin seeing the people and places about whom I'm writing as flesh and blood. They wear clothes and eat food, and if I'm lucky, I hear them laugh. I'm so very much there.

Which is a gift . . . and a huge setback when it comes to relationships with people in this moment, now. Fortunately, I have friends who get it and who pull me out of the records to get hazelnut gelato.

I slowly ate my extra-large cup of goodness while Marcie and Nicole talked about meeting some of the guys from VMI in the coffee shop that morning, about how the guys had tried to pick them up. "It was enough fun just to see their faces when we said we were in

high school, but then, when we held hands . . ."
I felt a smile ply my lips. I would have liked to
have seen that.

I was staring out the window at the
buildings across the street. I wondered how old
they were. Had they been around when Obadiah Popson had lived? Had he come to Lexington to shop? How far would that have been?
A day's ride? Would he have brought any of his
slaves with him? Would they have needed a
pass? Was that a treat or a burden, to get to
leave the farm for a day or two?

I saw a wagon come up the road in front
of me, its wheels spoke-deep in mud. At the
reins, a black man steered two red horses toward the side, and a white man jumped down
from the seat beside him. "Wait here. I'll be
back momentarily."

The white man stepped up onto the
high, wooden sidewalk beside the wagon and
disappeared through an open door, where I
could see stacks of cans and the hint of a counter. A mercantile?

The man on the wagon sat still, barely
seeming to move. But I could see his eyes.
They were scanning the scene before him—
men in dusty clothes moved between the
buildings, and a young white woman with two

children passed in front of the wagon without a glance at him. Across the street, two black teenage girls moved quickly on the sidewalk, their heads down, a white woman in an elaborate green dress ahead of them.

I thought I saw the man on the wagon smile. Then, the white man sat back beside him and dropped a crate of goods behind the seat. "The blacksmith."

The black man clicked his tongue and flicked the reins, and they were off down the road and out of my sight.

I startled when something moved right in front of my face. Javier's hand.

"Mary, are you with us? Mary, come back to the gelato."

I felt my cheeks flush and looked down at my bowl full of slightly-runny goodness. Then I glanced up at my boyfriend and friends from beneath my eyelashes. "Sorry, guys. I was just—"

"So what did you see?" Marcie asked. Only a best friend would help avert your embarrassment by engaging in it. She was used to my daydreams.

I told them about the men on the wagon, about the way the street had looked.

"Oh, I saw old pictures of this street at an art gallery up the road. Want to look?" Nicole almost shouted.

Now, if Nicole wasn't in love with Marcie, I'd think she was trying to woo me. Old pictures of places I knew were just about my favorite thing in the world. I shoveled the rest of the gelato into my face and savored the burn of the ice cream headache, then followed my friends out of the shop.

We walked past cute storefronts all decorated with early spring goodies. At this time of year, we were all optimistic about flowers. Nicole led us into a corner shop where all the trim was painted barn red. Inside, photographs hung in simple wooden frames and prints were laid in bins for people to peruse.

"Here," she said in that voice we all use for art stores and museums. "See?"

I stared at pictures of VMI—almost the same even down to the uniforms—and then of Terra Linda. There was the old hardware store in its heyday. A whole group of men was on the porch, and through the windows, I could see bins and shelves full of what I assumed must be nails and screws or whatever they used to build with back in the day.

Here was Charlottesville, the Downtown Mall a bustling street full of cars. The label said, "1935." And here the old Rockbridge County High School that was now the county offices for the school district. It looked the same, too, except in this photo there weren't any roads at all. Just a wagon or buggy pulled up right on the grass.

"Look," Marcie pointed me to a wall labeled "Lexington" with one of those stencils you stick right on the sheetrock. I saw the courthouse and some of the older houses up on the hill. And here was Main Street. The building we stood in was there, but the Coca-Cola mural on the side was vibrant then.

And then, there, was the mercantile I'd just imagined. It was exactly how I'd seen it, down to the white cans in the doorway. In front of it, there was a wagon—a black man driving and a white man beside him. I stared and leaned in. It was the two men I'd just imagined. Same clothes. Same postures. Same horses.

The caption read, "Obadiah Popson from Terra Linda."

I dropped my mittens on the floor and gasped.

Javier took two strides from across the gallery and looked from my face to the photo and back. "What, Mary? Are you okay?"

Nicole and Marcie made their way over, too.

"You won't believe this, but this is what I just saw."

They stared at the picture and then returned their eyes to me. "What do you mean?" Javier took my hand.

"When you all were talking back at the gelato place, I saw this happen. I saw the wagon pull up. I saw these men. Just like they are in this photo."

"Hmm." Marcie said with a smile that masked the slight look of fear I could see at the corners of her mouth.

"But you don't understand. That man there." I used my pinky to point at Popson without touching the glass that covered the image. "That's Merle Popson's great-great- grandfather, Obadiah."

I was too stunned to move, but I did notice a quick glance pass between Javier and Marcie. Javier slipped an arm around my waist and moved me toward the door. Before I knew it, I had a cup of hot chai in my hands and was seated at the back of the coffee shop next door to the photo gallery.

"Drink," Marcie said. "Drink first. Then tell us."

I took a sip and then blew on the liquid. Another sip, and then I told them about what I'd found in the clerk's office. I showed them the Popson family tree I'd drawn and then the notes about the slaves that Obadiah Popson owned.

"One of these five men was the man on that wagon."

We all sat in silence for a while, our drinks passing from table to lips slowly and with care.

"Alright, we know that you don't see things, Mary, for no reason. So your vision— and then that photo—you are supposed to know that. Any idea why?" Javier held my hand as he spoke.

I stared at the barista behind the counter, grateful that my friends had chosen a seat near the rear of the shop so that I couldn't really see out the window. I'd seen enough of that street for the day.

"I have no idea."

"I'll be right back," Marcie said as she slid her coat on her arms and made her way to the front door and out.

I didn't know what to think. I'd gotten used to seeing ghosts—well, as used to that as a person could get, I expect—but seeing into the past. That was different. We lived in a place where history was people's every day conversation, and I didn't know how it would be for me to slip into seeing then at every corner. I mean, I saw stuff a lot—and until now I'd thought it was just my imagination—the image of an old farmer on his horse-drawn plow by Singing Waters farm just down the road from our house, or the little girl with ringlets I'd seen in front of Neriah Baptist one time. Once I'd watched an entire marching band walk down Main Street in Terra Linda. Then, there was that photo of the murders that had seemed so real. I'd just thought it was my imagination. Had I been seeing things I needed to attend to? The idea made my heart hurt.

Just then, Marcie came back in with a small package in her hands. "Here." She handed it to me.

Inside, there was a small version of the picture of Popson. And on this version, the caption read, "Obadiah Popson and his boy Ned."

16.

It would be understating to say I was confused and baffled, maybe even a little bit
honored, too. I now had these two gifts—
and that was a term I was willing to pick up
only sometimes—and I wasn't sure what I
needed to do with them. I wasn't even sure I
wanted them.

I'd heard that parable about the talents
enough times to know that God doesn't hand
people something—a skill, a desire, a dream, an
ability—and willingly accept that they don't use
it. But I was hard-pressed to know how. What
does one do with the ability to see ghosts and
the ability to catch glimpses of the past?

More specifically, what was I supposed
to do now that I knew about Ned?

After dinner, Mom and I took opposite sides of the couch, mugs of hot cocoa with lots of marshmallows in our hands, and talked it through. Well, mostly I talked. She listened. What with the couch, it kind of was like therapy. That was okay with me.

"So then, Marcie handed me that photo." I took a swig of my now tepid drink. "But I don't know how to pull all this together. I don't know what I'm supposed to do." I felt tears sting my eyes, and I knew I had touched on the heart of the truth for me. Tears were always my indicator.

Mom looked at me closely for a few moments, and I stared at my marshmallows. You'd think I'd be used to that gaze of hers, the one that is equal parts about seeing me and about reading her own heart, but I wasn't. It always made me squirm a bit, not to get away, but to settle in.

"That picture. Wow. Yeah, that's something." She picked it up from the coffee table where I'd laid it. "Well, you know who Obadiah is, and you know how he's connected to what we're doing now, and more specifically to Charlotte and the twelve children. So I'm not sure it's really a question of what to do, but when." I felt her eyes come back to my face.

My stomach sank. She was right. I knew what needed to happen, but I didn't relish the thought of doing it. "Yeah." I stretched a heavy sigh across the room. "I'm sort of tired of being the one to bring things into the light." I set my mug on the table and pulled my legs close to my chest.

"I know."

We sat that way until I fell asleep.

On Monday, I asked Javier to drop me off at Shady Run instead of taking me home. He offered to stay with me, but I needed to be alone with the past.

I took the key out from the lockbox Micah had secured to a fencepost behind the school and let myself in. Then, I turned off the lanterns that we left on for the sake of security, and sat down in a desk beside Charlotte. Really, I wanted to curl at her knees like the children did, but figured that wasn't appropriate. She was, after all, just a couple years older than I was.

We sat in the darkness together for a while and listened to the children's marbles clack and the scratch of chalk on the board.

"You okay?" I finally asked.

"Yes, ma'am. You?"

"Sort of."

It was a quiet place, peaceful, which I know is ironic given that thirteen dead people lived there, but it was true. There's something about the places of the dead that I find restful, at ease.

I told Charlotte about the trip to the clerk's office, about my vision, about the photo. I set all that weight out there and let it rest like so many clothes draped over the children's desks.

Gently, Charlotte stood and began to walk around the room in a way that I now knew was her thinking walk. I watched her amble from desk to desk, her hand grazing across the wood. I lay my head on my crossed arms and closed my eyes.

I woke up when Charlotte placed her hand on the center of my back between my shoulder blades. I had no idea how long I'd been asleep, but I was the most rested I'd been since Friday.

She sat down next to me and turned her desk so we were facing one another. "I don't think you do anything, Mary. Not right now, at least."

I started to protest, to tell her that the weight of carrying this information was too great for me alone, that I needed to share it. But she looked me directly in the eyes, and I knew she was right.

"The time will come," she said, "when you'll need to tell. But for now, let me help you bear up under this story. We'll carry it together."

I gave her a wan smile and looked away. I didn't need to have her see me cry. She was the one who needed justice, and here I was feeling overwhelmed by some facts, facts that didn't have anything to do with my life, at least, not directly. I wanted to be able to push them away, but even as I thought that, I knew I'd be wrong. What hurt anyone, hurt me, too.

I turned back, and Charlotte's face was soft in the light of the dusk. She was looking at me with a question, and the question wasn't about whether I'd accept her advice or not. It was about whether she had overstepped, gone too far into our friendship.

"Thank you, Charlotte," I whispered. "Thank you."

A band of light flashed across our faces, and we blinked. Micah stood in the doorway, and his eyes were wide. I had scared him.

"Micah, I'm so sorry. I just came in here to talk to Charlotte a while. I didn't mean to be here so long. I'm sorry I scared you."

He let out a long breath. "No, Mary. You're fine. Just you and Charlotte there in the dark like that. I thought maybe you'd turned ghost, too."

I smiled. "No, sir. Still a living girl here."

He folded himself into the desk in front of me and then spun it around. "What are we learning today, Miss Braxton?"

"Today, we're learning about waiting."

For the next few weeks, the parents of Shady Run got busy. They started a major fundraiser to get the roof replaced and have electricity run, and they raised the money in five days. Then, they petitioned two local garden centers to donate plants, which they did— in droves. So I spent a lot of afternoons there planting bushes and trees. My favorite was the Japanese maple that we placed just under the front windows.

We finished up with the painting, inside and out, and installed a working pipe chimney, donated by the hardware store in town, to work where Darren's antique stove had been. The floors got refinished, and Darren put his hand to a new bathroom in what used to be the coatroom.

When the building was looking brand-new, Isaiah built a slim wooden frame on the wall that you saw when you came in the room, and Micah had a blue board so that the parents could hang pictures of the children and Charlotte there. Each portrait was framed in gold, and beneath every image, someone carefully hung a silver plaque with the person's name and birth and death dates. Charlotte's image hung in the middle. Once I caught her staring at herself. I wondered what it must have been like to see yourself for the first time in over fifty years.

Finally, someone—I never knew who—replaced that pane of glass where the hose had come in. When you looked really close, you could see the date—October 7, 1954— carved into the corner.

Meanwhile, Mr. Meade's classes had taken on another research endeavor: a genealogy on Charlotte and the twelve kids. They were trying to put together comprehensive family trees for each of them. My notes from the clerk's office gave them a bit of a head start. I, however, was quietly doing the same project, but for Bud Granger and Merle Popson. I had told Mr. Meade about what I'd found in the clerk's office—deciding to leave out the photo, since it seemed to be off-topic at that point—and he'd tasked me with seeing if I could find the same kind of info on Tomlinson and Granger.

Granger's line was a snap. Merchants and business owners since Terra Linda had been founded, their family history was easy to find in not only county records but the newspaper, too. In terms of slaves, his great-great-grandfather had owned two—one man and one woman. "House servants" probably, which made sense, since the Granger's had never been farmers.

Tomlinson's tree was really small because I didn't have access to international research materials. His grandparents on both sides had emigrated from England in the early twentieth century. I could have asked Shamila for her login to dig more, but I knew that anything we found there, while interesting, wouldn't be relevant to the larger project.

The Popsons had been in Virginia since it became Virginia, I learned. Merle's great-great-great-great-grandfather had come over in the early 1600s, not long after the Jamestown colony was reestablished. They had, as I would learn later in my life, followed the migration pattern of most wealthy Virginia families and moved slowly westward until they ultimately settled in Terra Linda, where they had been able to buy enough land to establish their wealth more or less permanently.

Along the way, they had acquired slaves. From what I could see in the tithable records—the notes about what tithes the Popsons had paid to the Church of England in the 1700s—they had "owned" eighty adult human beings. (I hate using the word "owned" because, well, people can't really own other people. We can oppress and enslave. We can subjugate, but we can't really own.) By the time I found them again on the 1850 census, the family was enslaving over 120 people, and thus, they were one of the wealthiest families in all of Virginia. In fact, they had owned more people in Rockbridge County than anyone else that year.

You see, where I live is pretty mountainous. There's not much good agricultural land, except in a few of the valleys and along the Maury River. So while people certainly kept slaves, they didn't keep many. A couple to work in the house, maybe, or a dozen or so people to work the little patches of land that grew their food and a little bit of crop to sell.

Shamila helped me understand all of this one afternoon at the Historical Society. It was just beginning to snow outside, and I was settled into one of the big wingback chairs in the front of the Society building. I kind of like the idea of being snowed in with Shamila in this great big house, so I was dawdling—that's what Mom would say I was doing, anyway.

Across from me, in the matching chair, Shamila was talking to me about slavery, about the different ways it looked in Virginia and then in other places in the South. This was her specialty, and I loved listening to her talk. Her eyes got shiny—sometimes with tears—but more with the energy that comes when someone shares work they want to give their heart to. I didn't always understand the specifics of what she said, but I understood her commitment to these people.

"So here, most enslaved people did other kinds of work in addition to working the fields. That was true for some folks on every plantation, but here it was especially true, since there wasn't really enough farm work to keep everyone busy. Around here, a lot of slaves were hired out further south or back across the mountain. That way, their masters didn't have to feed and clothe them but they still made a little money off of them. Or they did other work like quarrying or mining."

"Then, at the Popson place," I finally asked with an eye toward the inches of snow gathering outside, "what did they do there?"

"Well, we can't know for sure unless we find their papers, and I'm looking, believe you me. But I expect they did farm some, down there on that bottom land by the river. Probably tobacco, I expect. Maybe wheat. But I imagine that they were also skilled workers, too, probably bought from plantations back east and brought over. A blacksmith, a carpenter, maybe someone who could weave. A shoemaker, maybe."

I thought I was catching on now. "Ah, so the Popsons could have all that stuff made for them without paying to have it made, right?"

"Right. But also they could take in work that those people would do. Popson may have had the only blacksmith in town, and so people would have paid him to have that man do the work. I've seen plantations where an enslaved man ran a sizable business bringing in work from across the county. Sometimes, that made his owner very wealthy, and not just land or people rich, but cash rich. That was rare."

The snow had started to cover the roads, and I knew that if we didn't head out then, Shamila and I really would be stuck. "I guess I better go."

"Get your coat. I'll drive you home."

We talked more on our quick but cautious drive to my house, and when we got there, I tried to convince Shamila to stay over. She had to drive all the way to Lexington to get home, and it was getting bad out.

"Thanks, Mary. But I'll be okay. I plan to spend tomorrow with a good book, a cup of tea, and a soft blanket."

"Text me when you get home."

"Sure." She backed out of the driveway and headed down the hill.

Part of me had wanted her to stay. A slumber party sounded like so much fun, but another part of me wanted to sit with what she'd taught me today. A big Popson plantation right there on the river—Shamila had been able to find the place on the Hotchkiss map made in 1861. I knew right where it had been. Now, an elementary school stood there, but the land around it—all along the Maury River—was still open. When the snow cleared, I thought I'd take a walk there.

Tonight, though, I had some more research to do.

The next morning, I woke to over eighteen inches of snow—a lot for a March storm—and didn't even bother looking to see if school was cancelled. In Virginia, even in the mountains, snowflakes caused a panic, and this much snow, well, it might be a county-wide emergency. I was in for the day.

I wandered down the stairs to find Mom, of course, already in the kitchen cooking breakfast. We had kept power by some miracle, and I could smell bacon. I dropped into a kitchen chair and grabbed for the mug of coffee Mom had made me—super creamy and super sweet.

"You were up late last night. I saw the light under your door."

I swigged from the delicious nectar. "I can't find more information about the Popsons. I'm trying to see if there might be plantation records somewhere."

"You looked at VMI and at UVA?"

"Yep. Nothing. I couldn't even find many books that mention them, except in passing. You know, stuff like they were at this wedding or that one of the men voted this way in that election. It's weird. Most of these big Virginia families gave all their papers to a library or something so that they'd be preserved, but I've looked everywhere—the Library of Virginia, the Virginia Historical Society, even William and Mary. Nothing."

"I wonder if they might still have them, kept them as part of their own family collection." She laid two scrambled eggs with cheese and two pieces of bacon in front of me. "Maybe you should ask Mr. Popson."

I rolled my eyes to the top of their sockets and looked at her through my eyebrows. "Really? I can see how that would go. 'Hi, Mr. Popson. Remember me? I'm Mary Steele, the girl who wants you to confess that you murdered thirteen people. I was wondering if you had any old family papers that I could maybe look through.' I'll be lucky to not be shot off the front porch. No, I don't think that's going to work."

Mom shrugged. "Yeah, maybe you can't ask, but I bet Blanch can."

Blanch Perry had come to my rescue more than a couple times in the past few months, because he was a nice guy, but also because he'd had a bit of a crush on me. Now, though, he was dating Kimberly. I wasn't sure he'd be quite so keen to help . . . and I'm not so sure Kim would be keen on having him help.

"You won't know until you ask," Mom stated. Why did she always have to be so reasonable?

After breakfast and a little bit of *The View*, I picked up my cell and texted Blanch. "You got a minute?"

His reply came back almost instantly. "Yep."

I gave him a call. "Hey. How are you? How's Kimberly?"

The silence was a bit too long. "Oh, we broke up. She wasn't into history, and you know me, I'm all about history."

"Most Likely to be a Historian" is not what I expected to see by Blanch's yearbook picture, but okay. I sighed. "I'm so sorry. You okay?"

"Oh yeah. I'm fine. I broke up with her. How's Javier?"

Was that a hint of snideness in Blanch's tone? That so wasn't him. "He's great. We're great," I stressed. Best to make things clear here.

"Oh. Well, what's up?" The guy sounded sad.

"Well, I was wondering if you were up for an adventure . . . with me." I felt kind of bad adding that last part, but I needed his help.

"Anything for you, Mary."

Oh, I wished he didn't sound so forlorn, so like a beleaguered knight from a fairy tale. Still, I needed his help.

I told him about what I'd found about the Popson family and about needing to know if they had any family records. "But I can't very well ask him."

"Right. The school and the murders and stuff. Gotcha."

"So I was wondering—"

"I'll call him when we get off. Tell him I have a school project and was wondering if they had anything I could look at, anything exclusive."

I hoped I wasn't reading too much into Blanch's voice, but it sounded almost like he was excited. "And you're sure you're okay with this? He won't be happy when he finds out you shared anything with me," I said.

"Who says I'm going to share?"

I started to protest, but then I realized he was teasing. "Ha. Ha. Very funny."

"No, Mary, it's fine. It's for a school project, right, so you're bound to find out. And I won't even be lying. I still need something to do for Mr. Meade's final, right?"

Mr. Meade let students do major research projects instead of taking final exams. Well, we still had to take the final, but he just took the higher of our two grades—and the grades for the projects were almost always higher—and used that in his final scoring for the class. It was awesome.

"Right. Well, then, thanks, Blanch."

"Really, Mary. It's nothing. Thanks for calling. I'll let you know what I find out."

I hung up feeling a little slimy, but also excited.

Within the hour, Blanch had called to say he was going to the Popsons' house this afternoon. "A perfect excuse to take Dad's truck out in the snow."

Blanch was a good friend, and I had to admit taking a ride around in this mess sounded kind of fun. But of course, I couldn't go, for a couple of obvious reasons.

I tried to stay busy through the afternoon. I cleaned my entire room, including the closet, and returned all the dirty dishes—three spoons, a bowl, and two plates caked with some substance I did not want to identity—to the kitchen. I threw away a million scraps of paper that had once seemed so important for me to keep. I organized my bookshelf, first by subject and then alphabetically within subject . . . and still it was only one fifteen. Have I mentioned that I hated being bored? Still do.

Finally, I curled up in the recliner with a cross-stitch project I'd started about five years ago—a chickadee on a branch with red berries—and turned on Netflix. Mom joined me, and we finally settled on a *Ghost Adventures* marathon. It seemed fitting.

As we watched Zak Bagans and his team set up their equipment and then over-dramatize the danger involved in what they were doing, I thought about Charlotte and Henrietta and the other kids. I knew they couldn't feel cold, but still, it must be lonely over there on a day like this when no one can come by, when it seems like, once again, everyone has forgotten you. I wished I could get over there, but Mom's Prius just wasn't cut out for the snow. Javier said it was barely cut out for the road at all.

Just as episode five of our marathon was about to begin and I was putting the final stitches in the chickadee's wing, someone knocked at our door. Isaiah had been planning to try and come over for the evening, so we thought it was probably him. But when I opened the door, there stood Blanch with a grin as wide as the doorframe.

I stared, then smiled, and ushered him through the door and out of his coat and boots. Mom got him a hot cocoa, and we settled in at the kitchen table.

I was fairly bursting to know what Blanch had found, but I knew it would be impolite for me to push. I could almost hear Mom say, "Let the boy finish his cocoa first, Mary Steele." So I waited with one knee bouncing under the table.

Finally, Blanch ran the back of his hand over his mouth and let out a huge sigh. (He was kind of adorable.) "He has papers. Lots of papers."

"What kind of papers?" My voice was all squeaky.

"Mostly letters, but also some books— 'farm journals' he called them. Want to see them?"

Mom and I looked at each other, then at Blanch.

"They're all in my truck outside."

"Good gracious, son. Let's get those things inside." Mom was already halfway into her coat.

When we pulled back the tarp on Blanch's truck, I saw the bed full of boxes. At least twenty of them. "He just let you take these?"

"Yep. Well, after I told him that I'd sort them and label them and send him an inventory."

"Blanch! That's a ton of work."

"I knew I'd have help." He grinned at me.

Of course he would. I couldn't resist going through all these. He knew that.

We loaded all the boxes into the living room, and Mom brought up a folding card table from the basement. This wasn't going to be a one-night project, and we all knew Blanch couldn't take these things home. His daddy didn't take kindly to all his "history nonsense," and his three-year-old sister didn't promise to treat the nonsense kindly, either.

Mom dragged three chairs in from the kitchen, and we all took a box. "How do we want to do this?" she asked.

"Is there any order to what's in here, Blanch?"

"Nope. Just piles of paper."

"Alright, so I think what would be best is if we sorted things by date. Maybe a pile for each year? Then we can put the years in order

. . . that's how the boxes at the Historical Society are organized," I suggested.

"Makes sense." Blanch nodded and opened his box.

I grabbed my phone and sent a group text to everyone: "Blanch just scored us all the Popson family papers. If you can make it over, come to my house and help us sort them."

It turned out that no one else could get up our hill, although Javier tried. I could imagine the tires on his Nissan spinning. He knew how Blanch felt about me, and while he trusted me, he wasn't terribly keen on me spending a snowy evening by the fireplace with the guy. "I can't make it, girl," his text said. "I miss you, though."

For the next six hours, we made stacks all around the living room. We had documents from 1773 up until the 1960s—everything from receipts to the letters Blanch had mentioned to draft cards to books. Eventually, when some of our towers began to teeter, we just took everything out of the boxes and put it on the table and then began to put the largest piles into the boxes by year.

By the time it reached eleven o'clock, my eyes were burning from trying to make out tiny letters and from dust, and Blanch looked like he could fall asleep on the table. But Mom was still sorting away, her feet shuffling from pile to pile like they were made of wheels.

"Mom, I think we need to quit for the night."

"Oh, okay, honey. You guys go on to bed."

Blanch's head popped up, and Mom didn't miss that.

"Mr. Perry, Mary will get you a pillow and a blanket, and you can sleep on the couch." She gave me a pointed look and I hurried to the linen closet upstairs.

"Thanks, Mrs. S. I'll let my mom know I'm sleeping here. I don't reckon the roads are great yet."

"I expect the ice is bad, since we had a little melting, and since they've already cancelled school for tomorrow, I don't see that it does any harm for you to stay here."

"Yes, ma'am."

I threw his pillow and two blankets on the couch and gave Mom a hug. Before I went to sleep, I texted Javier. "I miss you, too. Come over tomorrow morning if you can." I hesitated but figured it was better he know beforehand. "Blanch is sleeping on the couch, and we're going to finish sorting tomorrow."

The text took a bit longer than I'd hoped. "Okay."

"I love you."

"Yeah, I love you, too."

17.

I woke to the sound of knocking at the front door. A quick look at the clock told me it was only six thirty. No school, and someone was knocking at 6:30 in the morning. Gah!

I climbed out of bed, and remembering that Blanch was downstairs, pulled on some sweatpants and a bra.

Mom was just ahead of me on the stairs, and as I passed through the living room, I could see Blanch stretching on the couch.

When Mom cracked open the front door, Isaiah stood there with a box in each hand—one of coffee and one of donuts. I knew why Mom loved that man.

"A little early, I know," he said. "But I couldn't wait to see what you'd found."

Behind him, I saw a familiar car slide up to the curb, and Javier moved slowly up the walk. I let Isaiah in and then stepped out onto the stoop, closing the door behind me.

"Hi."

"Hi." His voice was brusque, and he looked like he hadn't slept at all.

"Hey." I looked up into his face and smiled.

"You okay?"

"Yeah, I'm fine, well, except for waking up at the butt-crack of dawn on a snow day."

That got a little smile.

I stepped closer and wrapped my arms around his waist. "It's only you."

"Yeah? I couldn't get here last night, and I felt awful."

"I know. I wanted you to be here. How'd you get here this morning?"

"I dug the car out for a few hours last night, and then my brother helped me push it out our lane today. I came in the back way to get here so I wouldn't have to climb this hill."

"You did all that for me?"

He blushed. "Well, and for me, too. I was a mess all night."

I couldn't help but be flattered. Jealousy is not a desirable trait when it makes someone possessive or mean, but it could be kind of sweet when it makes a guy all discombobulated for you.

I moved forward and kissed him softly for a long moment and then broke away.

Inside, the coffee was already in mugs and the donut box open on the kitchen table. I grabbed a Bavarian Cream for myself and handed Javier a chocolate frosted. I never would understand why he didn't like cream-filled goodness, but he hated it.

We all sat around on the floor of the living room and kept our donuts away from the papers. If Shamila were here, she'd probably have laid plastic over everything in the night, but we weren't archivists, so the best we could do was to try to avoid adding powdered sugar to the dust.

As soon as we'd all eaten, we began the sort again after briefing Javier and Isaiah on the system. We worked slowly and deliberately, and everything went great. Javier and Blanch managed to simply not be near each other, and I was grateful for that. I tried to keep my head down and focus.

By the time Marcie, Nicole, Shamila, and Mr. Meade made it up from town around ten, we had all the papers sorted by year with a BIG group of "n.d." papers in two boxes at the side. I had felt a little smug when I'd explained that archivists use "n.d." to indicate "no date" on files. Sometimes, it's the littlest things that make us arrogant.

In fact, I was feeling pretty smug about the whole endeavor. I have a tendency—still—to start "taking charge," that's what Mom always said, when I feel like I've got something under control or, ironically, when I don't. Today, though, I felt like I was on top of it all, and so I started to assign tasks. "Marcie and Nicole, why don't y'all sort the papers from the twentieth century?" I gestured with a grand hand over to a set of boxes and piles. "Blanch, maybe you and Shamila can work on the n.d. files; see if you can start to piece together some dates for those?"

"Isaiah and Mom," I caught my mother's eye, and she was giving me one of those stares that meant, *it's time to stop talking now, Mary.* I looked around the room, and everyone was looking at me, not with contempt, but with a little bit of surprise and frustration. Nicole was giving me a "Yeah, *no*" look. I smiled weakly and said, "I'm sorry" before quickly sitting down on the couch.

Javier sat right next to me and slipped an arm around my shoulders to give me a quick squeeze.

Mom didn't give me another glance, and I was grateful, before she turned to Shamila. "Shamila, Mary got us off to a good start by suggesting we sort these into piles. What should we do next?"

"That is a good start." Shamila smiled at me. "And we do need to start sorting these into date order, but I wonder if it wouldn't help to first put together some of the facts we know about the Popson family. Mary, you did some work on that, right?"

You know you've found your people when they can reign you in without shame. I sat forward a bit from my sulk on the couch. "I did. Would it help if I got my notes?

"I think so," Shamila said, smiling again.

"I'll get a flip chart." Mom moved toward her counseling office at the back of the house.

Marcie stood and headed toward the kitchen. "Cocoa?"

"Yes, please," I shouted from the top of the stairs. My notes were still in my bedroom.

As I turned to come back down, Javier caught me at my doorway and gave me a soft, long kiss. When he was done, I felt a little

swimmy in the head, but also more grounded.
I've said these were my people, right? Well, this
guy, this guy was totally my person.

Within a few moments, we were all back
in our rhythm. I had drawn a really lopsided
family tree on a giant Post-it Mom had hung
by the fireplace. It showed Merle Popson's
family line as far back as I'd been able to trace
it.

Then, Blanch, whose artistic skills far
outweighed mine, sketched an outline of the
old Popson family land along the river. The
original outline of their property was in red,
and the present-day structures and roads he
added in blue: the elementary school, Long
Mountain Road, the chicken houses that sat
back from the road a ways.

I could see right away why Shamila had
us get this information up. Now, we were all
working with a structure—we knew people and
places, so the documents might have something to hang on. Her plan was much better
than mine, but of course, I didn't say that out
loud. I didn't need to. It was very clear.

"So," Isaiah said, "we're looking for information about what in all these papers?" He

didn't look exactly overwhelmed with enthusiasm at the idea of sorting through all that paper.

"Well, um, that's a good question." Shamila looked a little puzzled herself. "Mary?"

I couldn't believe it. These kind people had come all this way on icy roads to help me with something that they didn't even understand. They didn't know about the photograph yet, not even Mom. But it seemed time.

"The other day, we went to Lexington . . ." I told everyone the whole story with Marcie, Nicole, and Javier interjecting more details, and when I was done, the room was heavy with silence. It felt like those minutes on a TV show where the bomb is ticking down, but we didn't have any appropriate mood music, unfortunately. This didn't feel like a good moment.

I almost started to cry. It had been hard enough for everyone to come to terms with the fact that I could see ghosts, but now I was telling them I could see into the past. I felt like I'd just grown a third eye on my forehead.

But then, Blanch said, "Now, that is cool," and the silence broke open like a wave. I took a deep breath.

"She's done this for a long time, right Mrs. S?" Marcie said.

"I guess she has." She looked at me. "We just thought you had a great imagination."

"Yeah, that's what I thought . . . but I guess it's more than that."

"I guess so," Mr. Meade said over a hearty laugh. "I'll need to have you tell me some more about World War II for our lesson next week." He winked at me.

I wished it worked like that. My term paper would be a breeze then.

After the rumble of energy about my "gift," I said, "So I was hoping that these papers would help us know more about Ned." I set the picture of Ned and Merle Popson's great-great-grandfather on the mantel.

"Alright then," Shamila's voice bounced off the walls of our living room with authority. "So then, we want to look for any references to enslaved people. Probably those are going to be mostly in these journals, but maybe in receipts and letters, too. The fastest thing to do is to look for names. We know the names of most of the white people on the Popson place, so when you see those, you can skip them. But if you see another name—particularly just a first name, but don't count out people who have surnames—let's make a list here." She stuck another piece of paper to the wall. "If you have any dates with that person or any other facts, include them, too."

I looked around the room at my friends. They were ready.

I wasn't sure I was.

18.

Six hours later, we had made it through about half of the documents, and we had five sheets of paper with names and a few dates. Ned's name had only appeared twice— once in an inventory from about 1830—"Ned, boy – 12"—and the other in one of the account books where Popson says, "$3.00 to Ned for chickens." So we knew that Ned raised chickens. I wasn't much of a chicken person, but that kind of made me like him more.

Still, that didn't tell us enough to give us much of Ned's story, and while we'd been searching for his, we'd compiled dozens of other names—most of which were for other enslaved people at the Popson place. There was

years of work here to pull these stories together, Shamila said, and we weren't even done
going through the documents.

We had, though, begun to make some
order out of the chaos, and now, most of the
early documents—from the 1760s until about
the 1820s were sorted into date order. Shamila
promised to bring Blanch some archival boxes
and files from the Society so that he could or-
ganize the papers appropriately on the condition that he ask Mr. Popson if he would
consider donating the files to the Society when
he was done reviewing them.

"I don't know if he'll go for that, Ms.
Shamila, but I can ask."

"That's all I need, Blanch. Thanks."

We clearly couldn't just leave stacks of
paper all over the living room until we had
time to go through them, so Mom and I dug
some empty boxes out of the basement and we
used neon yellow sheets of paper to keep the
years separated and laid them in boxes. Then,
we stacked the boxes in the corner of the living
room so that we could continue to sort. Mr.
Meade had a couple of students who could use
a little extra credit, and Mom said it would be

fine for them to come by a couple of afternoons a week to help. It wasn't going to be an easy job, but it would get done.

The roads had cleared some in the sunshine of the day, so we ordered pizza and all slumped around the living room with sodas and even more cocoa while we waited for it to arrive.

"Mary, what do you think Mr. Popson is going to say when he finds out what you've been doing?" Isaiah asked.

"I expect I should prepare for some harsh words, maybe even threats again." I sighed.

Silence hung in the room like fog.

Then, a knock at the door made us all jump. After a second, Mom said, "The pizza delivery person."

She headed toward the door, and Marcie and I went into the kitchen to get paper plates. Pizza required a certain casualness, Mom always said.

I was just opening the cupboard when I heard a man's voice rising at the front door. The pizza guy wouldn't be yelling, that's for sure. I reached the door at the same time as Isaiah and just in time to see Mr. Popson lean back to punch Mom.

Blanch, out of nowhere, blocked his punch, and Javier tackled him to the snow beside our front walk.

I saw Nicole on her phone behind me even before I had time to ask. "Stephen, we need you at Mary's house. Now." She nodded at me.

Javier had tugged Popson to his feet, and now he and Blanch were holding him by the arms. But that wasn't slowing down Popson's tongue or his anger. Just now, it was directed at me.

"How dare you trick me into giving you my family papers? How. Dare. You."

Isaiah, ever calm, although I could see the red rising up his neck, said, "Mr. Popson, no one tricked you." He looked at Blanch.

"I didn't trick you, and Mary didn't either. I told you it was for a school project, and it is."

Mr. Meade stepped around me onto the stoop. "It is. This is Blanch's term paper project. We are just helping him with it."

"You know what I mean." Popson was flailing against Blanch's and Javier's arms, trying to get free, trying to get at me. "I don't want her touching my family's things."

Something about the way he said the word *touching* made me think this was about more than just what I had done with the cemetery last year. He said the word like I would make them dirty.

Shamila moved into the light of the doorway with Marcie beside her, and I saw confirmation of what I already expected. Disgust flashed across Popson's face, and I looked at my friends. Yeah, they saw it, too, and it broke my heart for them to witness this kind of hate . . . again.

We couldn't very well all stand in the cold, so carefully, Blanch and Javier maneuvered Popson into the house and then to a chair at the kitchen table. He grew very quiet, but I could still see the rage behind his eyes.

While we waited for Stephen, Shamila and I gathered up all of Popson's papers, being sure to keep them organized and in order. Nicole neatly labeled each box with the years inside, and I copied over the Popson family tree and taped it to the top of the box. Shamila and Marcie quietly took down the Post-it lists and slid them into Mom's office. Popson didn't need more fuel for his rage.

Just then, Stephen arrived. Marcie led him to Mom's office, and Mom, Blanch, and I followed. Javier and Isaiah stayed with Popson.

"So what happened, Mrs. Steele? Mary?"

Mom told him about the papers, about Blanch's project, about Popson. Stephen took notes and nodded. "That all sound right, Blanch?"

"Yes, sir." I could tell he wanted to say more, but Stephen's official tone and notebook kept him quiet.

"I need to talk to Merle. Alone." Stephen looked me straight in the eye.

While Stephen and Mr. Popson were in the kitchen, the rest of us stacked the boxes of Popson's papers—with the family tree on top—by the front door. Then, we sat around on the edges of the furniture and hearth and waited.

When Stephen came out from the kitchen, his face was lean and pale. He looked so tired.

"Blanch, Javier, I'll need you to load all those boxes into Merle's truck."

Popson came and stood beside him now. "Make sure you don't hide anything. I want it all."

Stephen glanced at him and then looked at me with soft eyes. "Is this all of it, Mary?"

"Yes, everything you let Blanch borrow is in those boxes. It's all organized by date now." I looked Popson dead on. "I even did your family tree and gave you a copy of it." I glanced over at the boxes.

"Good." Popson's voice was sharp and brittle.

"If you have any questions, Mr. Popson—"

"I don't need any of your help, girl. You just leave me and my family alone from now on."

I felt the tears leap to my eyes. The hatred in his voice. It was awful.

Blanch grabbed the first of the boxes, and all of us took another and laid them carefully into the bed of Popson's truck. He had one of those hard-top covers on it, the ones Javier always said were so ridiculous because you couldn't open then more than a couple of feet. But in this case, it was a good thing. The boxes and papers would be safe.

"Mr. Popson," Blanch's voice was quiet but solid. "How did you know I was here?"

Popson didn't even look at Blanch as he climbed up into the driver's seat. "I called your mama to see how the research was going and to see if you'd found anything interesting. She told me you were here."

He started the truck and backed out of the driveway so fast I could hear the boxes slam against the cab. His tires left black marks on the road as he headed back toward town.

Slowly, we turned and made our way back into the house, Stephen, too. Mom got the pizza out—the delivery guy had brought it while we were loading—and we all sat eating in silence for a few minutes.

"Mary, off the record, you did give him everything, right?"

"Yep. Every piece of paper that he gave Blanch got loaded into that truck. Not that he'd know it. He didn't even know what he had in there."

Stephen nodded. "Well, that may be a good thing, but it may also be a problem if he decides to make up that something was stolen. Hard to prove that, though, since he'd have to have some proof that something existed to claim you stole it." He took a bite of pizza. "Still, it could make some trouble for you."

The quiet held around the room for a few minutes more. I was upset—frustrated and scared and a little hurt—and part of me just wanted to send everyone home and watch *Firefly* with Mom. But another part of me kept thinking about those lists of enslaved people that were folded up in the top drawer of Mom's desk.

Shamila must have been thinking the same thing, because she caught my eye and raised her eyebrows.

I bolted up and headed for Mom's office door.

"What are you doing, Mary?" Stephen's voice was a little anxious.

"We gave him every slip of paper he gave us. But he couldn't take what we'd already learned."

Stephen stood. "Probably about time I go, then." He smiled and winked as he went out the front door.

19.

We didn't get much further that night. First names and a reference to a 12-year-old boy with chickens wasn't much to go on, even with the power of the Internet at our fingers. Still, we made a complete list of the names of the people who were slaves on the Popson places, and Mom photocopied the list for each of us.

Then, it was time for everyone to go home. Mom said so, and I was grateful. After everyone left – Javier made sure to stay longer than Blanch did – Mom and I made hot tea and sat side by side on the sofa, her arm draped over my shoulder.

"Mama?"

She squeezed me closer.

"Why does this keep happening to me? I mean I'm not anyone special. I don't know why I keep getting pulled into this stuff. This is hard."

Mom laid her head on mine.

"I kind of understand the cemetery now. Know why I was there at least, but this school. . . I just don't understand." I took a deep breath. "I don't want this."

I felt bad as soon as I said it. I loved Charlotte and Henrietta and the other kids. I was so glad I'd met Micah, even Darren. But all of this felt like too much for me. I wanted to be a normal teenager who was worried about zits and who spent the weekend at the mall or – okay – at the library. I didn't want to be the Virginia mountain version of Haley Joel Osmont and "see dead people."

"I know, Mary. I know that's true. And I know it's also not true. I see it, the way you spark when there's a mystery that can be solved on paper. I watched you today, you know." She sat forward and looked at me. "When you're looking at those old documents, you get this kind of focus in your eyes – like the kind a cat does when it sees a bird. You are fascinated. Entirely intent on what you're doing. It's very cool to see."

I had been staring at my hands, but now I looked up into Mom's face. It was soft and gentle, tender. I took a deep breath and laid back on the couch. "Tomorrow, I think I need to go up to the school and talk with Charlotte."

Mom placed her hand on my calf and squeezed. Then, we turned on *Firefly*, and I lost myself in the future for a while.

Javier and I drove straight to Shady Run when our last class let out. The days were still short, and we thought it best to not be there after dark, given Popson's behavior the day before. Stephen had texted me earlier in the day to say that Popson wasn't pressing charges against Blanch or us because we hadn't really stolen anything. And I knew, of course, that Mom wouldn't pursue anything about the attempted assault.

Still, that didn't mean it was over, and we saw evidence of that when we arrived at the school. A security company was hanging cameras at each of the corners of the building, and when we went inside, we saw that there were sensors on both doors and all the windows in case someone tried to break in. "Mom must have let Micah know what had happened," I said to Javier as we watched the men work.

Charlotte already knew about Popson's visit because Micah had filled her in, and she said the security system was Darren's idea. All the parents had agreed and chipped in. I hated to admit it, but I thought it was a good idea, too. We didn't want this building destroyed after all the hard work, of course, but more, I didn't know what would happen to Charlotte and the children if their "residence" disappeared. Probably not anything good.

Javier had to get onto to band practice, so he kissed me on the cheek and confirmed with me that Marcie was on her way. "She'll be here by 4:30."

After he left, I sat down beside Charlotte, but not facing her since we didn't need the security company guys totally confused or thinking I was insane. . . although sometimes I wondered.

"Are you alright, Mary?" she asked.

I looked at her for just a moment. "I am. I think I'm getting used to threats."

Charlotte's face turned down for a moment. Then, she nodded. She knew the feeling, I imagined.

"Right now, I'm just trying to figure out what's next. How do we help you and the kids?" Henrietta was doing the hair of one of the other girls, pulling the tiny curls back into tight braids. I could see the child's hair changing as Henrietta's fingers moved through it, but I could also see it was still just the same as it ever was, pink bobble beads and all.

The teacher sighed. "I don't know that there's anything you can do to help us, Mary. I thought maybe once the building was restored we might be able to move along. Or maybe when the children saw their parents on more time. But, well, that doesn't seem to be it either."

It was my turn to sigh. "And I was thinking if we could get your killers to confess . . . but now it seems like that chance might be gone. I'm sorry, Charlotte."

She looked at me from the corner of her eye. "You can still see me, right?"

"Um, yes."

"Well, then I don't think we should give up hope yet." She took a deep breath. "Tell me about what you found in Merle Popson's documents."

I pulled the sheet of names out of my pocket and laid it on the desk in front of me facing her. She leaned in and scanned the names.

"Oh, I know some of these folks. I mean, I know some of these names. The grandparents of the children, most of them."

"You can tell all of that from this list."

"Sure. See here? Billy and Susie. That was the Noah family. Their girls are Daphne, Marigold, and Hester. They're Lucy's grandparents, too." She pointed over toward the slightly plump girl playing with her doll in the corner. "And this man here, Demetrius. I only ever knew one man with that name. He lived over in a little house by the river, caught fish and sold them from a cart in town."

Henrietta had come over by now and was sitting on my knee. "N-ed," she read from the list. "Ned!! That's my granddaddy's name."

I had brought the photo of Popson and Ned by to show Charlotte one day, and I'd told her about my visions. She'd taken it all in stride, but I suppose if you'd been haunting a place for 50 years, someone seeing into the past wasn't a big deal. Now, though, THIS was a big deal.

Charlotte and I grabbed each other's eyes. "What do you mean, Henrietta?" Charlotte asked in almost a whisper.

"Ned. My granddaddy's name Ned."

I took a deep breath. "What do you re-member about your granddaddy?"

She smiled. "He always brought me candy and let me ride on his shoulders. And every night, I got to help him get up the chicken eggs."

I almost pushed the tiny child to the floor I was so excited. "Your granddaddy raised chickens?"

"Oh yeah, lots of them. His daddy taught him how."

I did some quick math, and it didn't work. Henrietta's granddaddy couldn't have been born in 1818 like this Ned.

"Know what else?" The girl's face was lit up with a smile.

"What?" I said with a laugh. I just couldn't be sad with her joy around.

"His daddy named Ned, too, and that Ned's daddy, too. . . and that's my daddy's name, too." She giggled. "They all has the same name."

I opened my eyes wide and stared at Charlotte.

"Henrietta," the teacher said. "What was their last name?"

"Same as mine. Jones."

The little girl jumped off my lap and ran over to her friends, and I practically fell out of the chair with happy laughter.

Charlotte's face went very still, and her eyes locked on mine. "Maybe this is the way, Miss Mary. Maybe this is the way."

I grabbed Charlotte's hand and squeezed.

That night at dinner, I barely sat down before I started talking. I told Mom about Henrietta's father and grandfather and great-grandfather. I told her, too, about the security system and about how Micah had come by at dark to turn on all the lights inside. "So I had Henrietta tell him about all the Neds." He'd laughed with that big belly laugh of his.

"And that's when I remembered meeting Henrietta's parents, Roberta and *Ned*," I said his name with about eight syllables.

Mom opened her mouth to say something, but I couldn't stop. "So this may be it, right, Mom? The key. Maybe we just need to talk about Mr. Jones' grandfather Ned, tell that story, and then they can all get free of that school."

This time, Mom took a drink of tea and looked at me. "Maybe."

I felt my stomach drop into my knees. That wasn't Mom's excited tone. That was the voice she used to give bad news. I hated that voice. "What?" I said with annoyance.

Mom wiped him mouth with her napkin and then shifted in her seat to look at me more full-on. "I think this is great news, Mary. You're helping the Jones' find out more about their family. That's really important." She took a deep breath. "Still, Mary, how are you going to tell the Popson family that one of the children they killed was a descendant of a man their family once enslaved?"

I dropped the forkful of spaghetti that had been headed toward my mouth. My stomach turned into a spiral of knots. I looked at Mom. "I'm not. I mean, why do they need to know? They don't care, and it might put the school in danger." I got up and walked to the window.

Mom stood and placed her empty plate on the counter. She bent to kiss the top of my head. "I'm sure you'll figure it out."

In some people's mouths, that phrase might have been an abdication of responsibility, a way of stepping out of the problem and shifting it entirely onto the other people's back. But I knew that's not what Mom was saying. I knew that she was just giving me time to think, time to let this all settle in. Time to eat my spaghetti.

I sat back down and stared at that table for a long while, trying to eat and trying to work my way through this problem. We didn't have any reason to bring people back to the school – it was preserved and the parents' were active. We didn't need a press conference or a big media spectacle this time.

As I dumped my spaghetti in the compost bucked, I pondered a fundraiser – something to draw the town in, something where we could dedicate the memorial to Charlotte and the twelve children. But I knew that wasn't my place. The parents should be the ones to do that IF they wanted to do it.

No, this time, our work had to be smaller, more private. Thirteen people had been murdered, and while that was a very public event, one that had left big wounds in our town, the work of healing here was more vast, deeper. Wider, too. And that made it harder. I had no idea what to do.

The next morning, when Javier beeped, I was sitting by the door. It's easy to be up early when you barely sleep.

On the ride to school, I told him about what we'd found out, about how I thought that was the key to getting Charlotte and the children some peace, and then about how I had no idea what I should do.

He listened and then sat quietly as we crossed into town. "Mary, what if you just asked Henrietta's parents what they wanted to do?" He said it so quietly I almost didn't hear him over the engine.

"So I would just tell them what I found?"

"Isn't it theirs to know? Theirs to decide what to do with?" He glanced over at me. "I mean, I know you want to do well and you care about our friends and those kids. But maybe this one isn't for you to decide."

I'd felt it as soon as he'd said it. Something inside my chest shifted over and up. But almost right away, I felt ashamed at my own arrogance. At my own pride. I was trying to take responsibility to fix something that wasn't mine to fix, at least not in the specifics. I let out a loud sigh. It wouldn't do any good to dwell on my own issues though. Javier was right. I leaned over and kissed him on the cheek.

That afternoon, I asked Javier to drop me at Shady Run again so I could see if Micah might be there. Charlotte said he'd stopped by earlier to check on things – nothing awry – and had gone home, she thought. I gave her a quick hug and then walked over to Micah's house.

He was in the front yard cutting down dried peony and mum stems. When he saw me, he laid the pruners on the front steps and took a seat on the porch, gesturing for me to join him. "What can I do for you, Mary?" His voice was quiet and kind.

"Well, Micah, I have some information, and I'm not sure who needs to know it. But I thought you might have some idea."

"Alright."

I told him about the Popsons's slave-owning history, the specifics of what we'd found in the Popson papers. Isaiah had told him, I knew, about the encounter with Merle Popson, but I wasn't sure anyone had caught him up on the documents themselves. I gave him a copy of the lists we'd created and then pointed to Ned's name.

"That's Henrietta Jones' great-grand-daddy, I think."

He stared at the paper a moment. "So then, Ned Jones is this man's grandson?"

"I believe so. I mean I can't be entirely sure without knowing the Jones' family tree, but it seems pretty likely."

He looked at me. "You asking me if we should tell them about this?"

I nodded.

"I would want to know, Mary."

"You would? I mean, you'd want to know that the man who killed your daughter was descended from people who owned your ancestor."

He took a deep breath. "Yes. I would. It'd be hard to know it, but I'd want to. It's part of their story, Mary. Part of who they are. And most of us," he gestured around to the cluster of small, low-slung white houses around us, "don't have much of that story."

I pulled my lips into a tight line and then let them fall into a frown. "Yeah."

He reached over and squeezed my arm. "Why don't I call them and invite them over for dinner? Maybe your mom can come, too? Or Javier?"

"Okay. That sounds good." My stomach was doing a full tumbling run, but it did seem the right thing.

"Friday night then. I'll let you know what they say."

I stood up and then bent back down just the few inches I needed to reach Micah's neck. "Thank you, Micah."

"Happy to, girl. Happy to." He looked up at me. "It's going to be okay. Now, don't you worry?"

I smiled then. If Micah thought it was going to be okay, then, well, I could make it to Friday without throwing up.

20.

On Friday evening, Mom and I pulled up to Micah's house. The Jones' car was there already. I took a shaky breath.

I'd brought all the documents I could find – including copies of the censuses that listed all the Ned Jones that Shamila and I could find and marriage certificates for Henrietta's parents and her dad's parents. It was clear that there were at least four generations of Edward "Ned" Jones, but it still wasn't possible to definitively prove that Ned, the man who had been enslaved by Merle Popson's ancestors, was Henrietta's great-great-grandfather. Because that man didn't have a last name, I couldn't definitely say he was the same Ned Jones I saw on the 1870 census. Or I couldn't

say that based on documents. The more I'd
thought about all of this during the week the
more I'd become sure that it was the same
man, if for no other reason than I had seen
both Henrietta's ghost and the image of Ned
and Popson back in early Lexington.

Still, I didn't know that my abilities to
see ghosts and peek into the past were things I
wanted to talk about tonight, much less use to
prove someone's ancestry.

We had a delicious dinner of beef stew
with Micah's homemade biscuits and a pan of
brownies Mom had made the night before. I
ate far too much out of sheer nervousness,
well, and because it was so good.

After dinner, we sat in Micah's front
room – the same one that Isaiah and I had sat
in when we first visited him – and sipped coffee and hot cocoa. It didn't take long for Mr.
Jones to get to the point. "This has been real
nice, Micah, but I expect you didn't just bring
us here to have dinner. What's going on?" He
said it with the most polite tone, but there was
a bristle underneath his gentle voice.

Micah looked at me and nodded.

"Well, Mr. and Mrs. Jones—" I began.

"Please, call us Roberta and Ned," Mrs.
Jones said.

"Um, okay, Roberta and Ned, well, I have some documents to show you." I spread the papers I had across the coffee table that Micah had cleared before we arrived. "I was able to track your family line back a few generations."

I walked them through the various documents from then to now, showing them how to read the marriage certificates and census records. They asked questions and listened as I answered.

When everything from the papers seemed clear, we sat back, and I asked the question I had been wondering. "Mr. – I mean Ned, Henrietta told me," it still felt weird to say that, "that your name was Ned, and her granddaddy's name was Ned, and his granddaddy, too. It looks like that pans out in terms of the paper trail, but I wonder if you can confirm that." I quickly added. "I mean, I don't doubt that Henrietta is telling the truth—"

"But she's six. No, I know what you're saying. Six year olds don't always get everything right." He smiled at me. "But in this case, she did." He looked over at his wife. "I can't believe she remembered that."

"I expect she's remembered a lot of things. 50 years is a long time to recall the stories of 6 years," Roberta said.

I gave them both a half-smile. "Okay, good, so then with your family's oral history and these documents, I think I can be fairly certain in saying that this man," I took the picture out of the folder beside me, "is your grandfather, Ned."

Ned quickly put his coffee cup down and took the picture. He stared for a long time at his grandfather's face, and then I saw his eyes slip down to the caption. I braced myself when I saw him wince just slightly.

"And this man, this man was his owner?"

"Yes. Yes, that man enslaved your grandfather."

The air in the room got very heavy.

"And that man's name was Popson?"

"Yes, sir. That was Obadiah Popson."

"As in . . . "

"Yes, that's Merle's Popson's great-grandfather."

The silence felt like smoke.

We all sat very still for a while. Ned passed the photo of his grandfather to his wife and then leaned back in this seat and folded his arms. I kept my head down and tried not to move.

After a while, Roberta laid the picture on the table, and I felt her gaze move to me. "I suppose, then, we know what we need to do to help Henrietta."

I looked up at her and then over at her husband. "We do?"

"We need one of those healing circles you do." Her voice was solid and straight as a heart-pine board.

I turned my eyes to Ned, and he gave me one, stiff nod.

The next morning, everyone gathered at the school house – Mom, Isaiah, Marcie, Nicole, Shamila, Mr. Meade, Javier, Blanch, Micah, Darren, The Jones, and me. The night before, we'd made a plan: we'd send personal invitations to everyone connected to the murders, inviting them to a time of forgiveness and transformation for the next Sunday afternoon. We wanted to personally hand people invitations or have a phone call with them directly so that we were sure everyone knew exactly what was going to happen – "We don't want anyone surprised here. It's better to have this out in the open since most of it is anyway," Roberta said.

This morning, we were gathering to decide who to invite and who would do the inviting. The first part of the invite list was easy since it included all the parents of the children who were killed and the few students who attended the school at that time but hadn't been there on that day. Then, we needed to invite "the accused," as Mr. Meade kept caling them, and we figured that it was only kind to suggest they bring their spouses.

It was the next part that got tricky. "We want this to be healing for everyone," Mom said during a quiet moment, "but I don't know. Does everyone need to be here to get that healing?"

"No, I don't think so. I think we need to keep it smaller." Mrs. Jones nodded her head as she spoke. "It's already going to be 30 or more people, possibly."

"I don't know. There's something mighty powerful about being witness to an apology, if one comes." Micah was staring at the front window as he spoke.

Isaiah spoke next. "Agreed. But then, what happens if it doesn't go well? The more people we have the more likely it is that something could get ugly quick."

I half-listened to the adults weigh all these things while I watched the children play in the corner. Charlotte was sitting with us, but her desk was angled – as it always was – toward the kids. Every once in a while, she'd turn toward them and watch for a minute, I presumed, to be sure no one was pinching or kicking anyone else.

After a few minutes, Javier shifted in his seat and said, "What about priests, pastors? What if we invited the ministers from two local churches – one white and one black – to be here? Maybe even the pastor from Granger or Popson's church? And Micah, the one from your church?"

I looked at the faces around the circle and saw them agree. "Sounds like a good idea," Micah said. "Might keep people a little calmer."

"Is everyone Christian that's coming?" Mom looked at Roberta.

"Christian or used to be."

"Granger and Tomlinson go to First Baptist, I think." I finally had something to contribute. "Popson. I don't know if he goes to church."

"Probably not." Shamila's voice was venomous.

I looked at her. Her jawline was rigid and her brow a scowl. Marcie reached over and laid a hand on her back. I saw Shamila take a deep breath.

"So that settles it." Darren had stood to stretch his back.

It wasn't as hard as I'd imagined to decide who would invite who. The Jones offered to contact all the parents, which seemed wisest, and Micah to talk to his minister. Mr. Meade said he could get in touch with the pastor at First Baptist, and Mom said she'd reach out to Granger and Tomlinson again. That just left Merle Popson.

I was staring at the desk in front of me, eager to let everyone else sort out this prickly bit. Maybe Blanch would do it? But suddenly, I sensed the room's energy shift in my direction and looked up to see everyone looking at me.

"What? No! You can't all think this is a good idea. He nearly punched Mom out, and he's furious with me. Blanch, can't you talk to him?" I bounced my gaze from person to person, and everyone – including Marcie, the traitor – was staring at me.

Javier took my hand. "Mary, it has to be you. You're the one that knows his family history best. You have the greatest chance of getting him to come."

"He's carrying around a lot of shame and heart-break, Mary. I've seen it so often when people find out their family owned slaves."

Shamila was leaning as far across her desk as she could. "The only way he can begin to let go of that is to confess it, not as his own choice but as his legacy, his responsibility." Her voice was softer now, but it was still tinted with anger.

I sank back against the wooden seat. "But how? I don't even know if I can get up to his house without being shot." I wasn't joking.

Everyone grew silent for a minute. "Work. Go to where he works." Nicole had been quiet until now, and of course, the one thing she had to offer was the reasonable option that might get me killed.

"I don't even know where the water department is." I heard the whine in my voice even as I said it.

"Mary Steele. With that smarty phone of yours, you can find anything." Micah smiled.

A chuckle passed around the circle.

Across from me, Charlotte was staring at the children again, her gaze intent but a little sad. It must be a weary life, if you could call it a life, to spend every minute of every day for over 50 years watching over children.

"Okay. I'll go on Monday after school."

As soon as the words were out of my mouth, I felt my stomach sink.

.

21.

On Monday afternoon, Javier and I sat in his car outside the public works building on the edge of town. I'd ridden past this place thousands of times probably, and never once had it seemed terrifying. Until today.

Popson, it turned out, was the Water Services Manager, the boss. Mom had looked him up on Saturday, and first thing this morning, she'd called to make an appointment for four o'clock.

It was 3:55 p.m., and I was fairly sure I was going to throw up. Again.

The last two days had both gone by at the speed of light and been as slow as molasses. I wanted this over with, and I never wanted it to happen. I hate that feeling and try to avoid it as much as possible by getting uncomfortable things behind me as quickly as I can.

But now, here I was with still four minutes to wait. I looked at Javier's watch again, and he kept my hand when I tried to pull it back.

"You're going to be okay. I'll be right outside if you need me. Remember, he's at his office. What can he do?"

It wasn't that I was worried that he would hit me or something. I knew, somehow, that his fist drawn at Mom was out of the ordinary. It was what he would say that had me shaking. Words do awful things, violent things, sometimes.

Still, I'd given my word, so I opened the car door and stepped out. I heard Javier's door slam behind him, but I didn't look back. I had to keep moving or I was turning around.

Inside, I told the receptionist I had a 4:00 p.m. appointment with Mr. Popson, and she directed me to have a seat.

A few minutes later, Popson came through the door, and I could tell instantly that I was not who he was expecting. Mom must have given him a fake name.

"Ms. Steele." His voice was ice-water-in-December cold.

"Hello, Mr. Popson. Thank you for seeing me." I knew that he wouldn't send me away, not with his receptionist right there.

"Follow me."

I watched his shiny shoes as we walked through a set of swinging doors and down a hallway to an office with a large metal desk and lots of bookshelves filled with rolls of paper. I couldn't help it—my curious nature really wanted to get a look at those plans, to see what they'd show me about our town. But I kept my interest at bay and took the seat he pointed to when we walked in.

I barely let him get seated before I started talking. "Mr. Popson, I'm so sorry about your papers. We didn't mean any harm. We just wanted to see—"

"Stop right there. You see the problem, don't you? I didn't give YOU those papers. I gave them to Blanch. They were none of your business."

I knew he was right. I had been underhanded in my curiosity, and it had made things worse. I wanted to justify myself, to say things

about the greater good and about history be-
longing to us all, but I thought better of it
when I saw his glare. "I know. I'm sorry."

He let out a deep breath. "Thank you.
Now what can I do for you today?" He wasn't
any less angry, but the decorum of his office
was holding him to some standards of behavior
that might not be so steady out in the rest of
the world.

I had come with the intention of simply
inviting him on Sunday and then leaving, but
now that I was here, I could feel other words
pushing up my throat and past my tongue. I
wanted to stop them, but I couldn't.

"I want to show you a picture, if that's
okay."

"A picture? A picture of what?"

I had the photo of Obadiah Popson and
Ned in a folder in my backpack, which I took
with me everywhere since it had my ID. I
slowly took out the folder, opened it, and then
turned it so that Popson could see the picture.
"That's your great-grandfather, Obadiah Popson."

He leaned in close and then picked up
the picture to study it. His gaze softened just a
little, for just a second. "Where'd you get this?"

"A friend bought it for me in Lexington." I realized that it wasn't helping my case that it looked like I was buying photos of his ancestors. "She just knew I liked historical photos."

He peered at me over the photo for a second and then returned his eyes to the picture. "I've never seen this picture. Is that Main Street in Lexington?"

"Yes, sir." I could feel myself getting excited, not because I had much hope for Popson's interest, but because history always made me feel that way. "You probably know the place. That building is across the street from the gelato shop. It looks a little different now because the road is higher."

He nodded and kept staring. Then, he quietly said, "Who's that man with him?"

I took a deep breath and held it. "That's Ned Jones, sir." I waited a moment ,but figured it was better just to spit it out. "He was your great-grandfather's slave."

I closed my eyes and braced myself for whatever came across that desk, but nothing came. Instead, when I opened my eyes, Popson's face had gone softer, and he had laid one finger on the picture.

"Ned Jones, you say. That was his name?"

"Yes, sir." A million questions were running through my mind. Did he know his family had been slaves? That they'd been "owned" by the Popsons? But I stayed quiet, sure that the work that needed to be done would be best served by silence.

We sat that way for a few moments. The silence rich and soft around us.

Then, he set the picture down and looked at me. "Thank you."

I shook my head a little to be sure I'd heard right, but then my manners kicked in. "You're welcome." I looked at him across the table. "I thought you'd want to have it."

"I do."

Again, I found myself unable to stop as I said. "There's something you might want to know." I gripped the handles of the chair. "Ned Jones' great-granddaughter Henrietta was in the school that day."

It took him a minute to understand, I think. At least that's what his face seemed to say as it moved from the wrinkles of confusion to the flat-skinned openness of shock and then, finally, to the tight-jawed stare of consternation.

But then, something behind his eyes gave a little—I know that description doesn't make much sense—but I saw something break free, something brittle and hard that had been cutting him open for years. He let out a long, slow breath.

We sat together then, the two of us, as the shadows deepened in the afternoon outside. I can't say how long we sat, really. And I wouldn't say it was uncomfortable. Rather, it was settled, resolute, accepting. I knew we were past the hard part now. Part of me wanted to think it would all be okay, easy from here on. But the most part of me knew that wasn't true, that hard things were still to come, as they always are, but in that moment, it was better, and sometimes better is all there is.

After quite some time, Popson looked at me and said, "It's never really been a secret. Not really. Everyone knows. I know that." He let a hard breath out of his nostrils and looked into the space above my head. "But as long as no one said anything, well, then I could pretend it was, well, I could at least keep it a secret from myself."

I sat very still and held my face soft. Now was not the time to get all righteous. Healing comes into soft things better than hard ones.

"I can't rightly tell you what we were thinking. Never have known that. 'Boys will be boys' is such a lame statement, but it was true. We were mad and got each other all worked up, and we'd had a couple of beers. It was the middle of the day—sky as clear as a summer lake. Not the kind of day for that sort of thing at all."

I got the impression that if this was a different kind of storytelling, he'd have leaned back and folded his arms behind his head. But he didn't. He sat with his elbows on his desk, stretching forward toward me.

"We were skipping school. We skipped a lot, bored mostly. Tired of being told what to do, I guess. I can't remember whose idea it was to go up there. Doesn't matter. Before I knew it, we were there. Then the hose. The window. The car."

I suppose some people would say I should have recorded what he was saying, taken out my phone and tapped for the voice memo. But I didn't think I'd need that. Didn't think it was right somehow—for him or for anybody.

"We only meant to knock them out. Scare everybody a bit. Put Micah in his place." As he said Micah's name, he raised his eyes to my face for the first time, drawn back to now by the living man, I guessed. "We was kids, though. Didn't know what we were doing." He huffed. "No excuse, though. I'm not wanting to make an excuse."

I believed him. Still do. This was confession, not explanation.

"When we found out what we'd done, we decided then and there never to talk about it again. We knew everyone would know, and we also knew that, things being what they were, we'd probably never get in trouble. So we took that and let it be."

I hadn't been angry until that moment. I understood what it was to do stupid things as a teenager, even horrible, stupid things. I could see how boys could make a terrible choice together. But to know with such confidence that they wouldn't get caught, *that* I couldn't abide. That society, that my town would be so blatantly hateful to some of its people that everyone could know thirteen human beings had been killed and nothing would be done—that made me furious.

Popson must have sensed my change of tone because he looked at me again. But he didn't speak. He just nodded.

I took a deep breath. There would be time enough for anger later. I still had a job to do here.

"Mr. Popson, I want to invite you to a gathering we're having at the school on Sunday. Just the parents of the children who died, a couple of ministers, and the three of you." I thought about explaining who I meant, but then, I figured I'd be playing like this was a secret again. We'd had enough of pretending.

He stiffened in his seat and glared at me. But as his hands shifted, he felt the photo still there and looked down at it. "What do you know about this man?"

At first I thought he was talking about his great-great-grandfather, but then I realized he was looking at Ned's face. "Not much," I said. "But I did see in your family documents that he had chickens."

He looked up at me quickly. "That was in those old papers? I didn't think there was anything worth knowing there."

I felt the corners of my mouth turn up. "Oh, there's always plenty worth knowing in piles of paper, Mr. Popson. Plenty."

He turned his gaze back to the photo. "Let me think on it."

It took me a minute to pull myself back from the quick illusion I'd conjured of having a chance to read more of those documents and realize we were talking about Sunday, about the most important thing. "Okay." I stood up. "If you decide to come, we'll be there at 2:00 p.m. Your wife is also welcome."

He stood, manners overriding all things, even fifty years of history.

I looked him in the face one more time and then turned and walked out the door.

22.

had no idea what Sunday would bring. We'd asked Stephen and some of the deputies to be onsite just in case, but we wanted them to stay outside in their civilian cars. As Darren said, "No need to escalate things before they get rising on their own."

We spent the next few days preparing—cleaning up the school again, making rich, baked things that could soothe spirits and tongues, getting together to plan the day, which really was more about comforting each other than it was about schedules and such. Sunday could go any which way, and we all knew that.

Still, the day arrived, same as always. It was cool but sunny, clear skies, and the hint of green on the tips of the trees. Spring was coming, sure enough.

Most of us, including the Joneses, arrived at the school about noon to set up. We had food to lay out and chairs to circle round. But we also needed to settle into the place, into each other. We knew we needed to hold each other up today, and it felt good, important really, to be in that space together, doing or pretending to do when the doing was done.

Charlotte and the children had gussied themselves. I could see it, even though they looked the same as they ever did. Still, there was a shine to them, brought on by washcloths or hope, I couldn't say.

Earlier in the week, Roberta and Ned had told Charlotte all about what was happening so that she could prepare the children. "Seems odd to ask someone else to tell my girl about what's coming," Roberta told me softly that day, "but then, she's known her longer than we did."

But we kept a bit of information to ourselves. Just before one o'clock, Lucille Braxton Clough walked into the school. I have her a hug at the door and then led her, as everyone else watched, over to Charlotte, who was just finishing up tying Isham's shoe.

As the schoolteacher rose to standing, I looked her in the eye and laid my hand on her arm.

The sisters saw each other in the same instant, and their faces moved from shock to joy to sorrow, as if mirroring the other.

I left them there, holding hands, and passed a hug to all the children as I went. We all needed to be seen today.

A bit before two, Stephen and his deputies arrived and parked around the lot, scattered so as to not draw attention. I watched as they leaned their seats back so that people wouldn't really notice them.

Micah had brought flowers from the local shop, and Mom was arranging them for the 400th time. Javier, Marcie, Tyrice, and Nicole were at the door to greet people, and Isaiah was shifting the chairs a bit, same as Mom with the flowers. Shamila had made a binder of information about all of the children and their families, and she'd included a special section about Charlotte after the two women had talked for a couple hours on Friday. The binder sat next to a stack of brownies on the table at the side of the room, and Shamila kept flipping back and forth amongst the pages. Darren was sitting quietly in a chair, and if I wasn't mistaken, he was praying. Or sleeping, but probably praying. Mr. Meade was ready to direct traffic and help people find parking spaces. Charlotte and Lucille were sitting knee to knee and speaking in whispered tones.

I was standing at the window, THE window, and watching. I was praying myself a little, too, for peace, for understanding, for honesty. For safety. I couldn't rightly tell you what I hoped would happen. Well, the idealistic, Pollyanna part of me was really hoping we'd get it all worked out, that everybody would forgive everyone, and we'd all go out for burgers later. But I knew that wasn't likely, or maybe, even the best thing. These kind of wounds take lots of time to heal, especially when they've festered this long—I knew that even then. So maybe what I hoped for was that people would speak truth and that they would listen to each other. Maybe I hoped this was a first step.

Folks began arriving right at two o'clock on the dot. Cars with Virginia tags and Maryland ones. A pick-up from Ohio. Each pulled in, and slowly, older, black couples climbed out and made their way inside. The ministers came together, and I imagined they'd had lunch after services and then prayed before they came.

Bud Granger was the first of the men to arrive. His wife came, too, both of them still in their Sunday best. Javier greeted them at the door with a firm handshake, and Marcie led them to the punch and snacks. They didn't look too nervous, but then, what does nervous look like after fifty years of hiding?

As the parents came in, they made their way to the corner where the children gathered, careful to sit and not draw attention to themselves or the kids. We'd all agreed that it was best that ghosts not be a factor in today's conversation, and I was very grateful. I did not want to be any focus of the attention today. Not in any way.

A bit after two, Stu Tomlinson came in alone. He found his way past Micah and shook his hand and went on over to the Grangers. They stood in a tight clump by the bathroom door.

At two fifteen, Isaiah gathered the group. "Welcome, everyone. We are so glad you are all here today. Thank you for coming. If you would, let's gather in the circle together."

I looked at Mom and shook my head. She nodded and sat down with everyone else. I lingered at the window a minute longer, but the street was empty. Stephen gave me a quick wave before I turned to join the circle.

I sat beside Mom and Lucille and studied the faces around me. None of us looked happy, none excited. *Beleaguered* was the word that came to mind.

"We all know why we're here today," Isaiah began.

I looked over at Charlotte. She was seated on her desk with her legs dangling. I imagined she sat that way many a day as she taught. We locked eyes for just a second, and she smiled. I felt my chest ease just a bit.

Isaiah continued with the directions for how the circle worked and brought out a true talking stick. He'd gone into Roanoke to a West African shop and bought a beaded gourd. We wanted something a little less charged than the baby doll, but still appropriate for the ceremony and the people gathered.

As we were set to begin, I heard the door open behind me, and from the corner of my eye, I saw Merle Popson take a seat next to Nicole. I gave him a small smile and tried to decide if this was good or not.

I saw Isaiah's eyes flit over to Popson and then quickly to me before returning to the half-focused gaze of someone speaking to a group, but not wanting to single anyone out.

"Our first question to consider today is what each of us remembers of the day that Charlotte and the twelve children died."

He passed the talking stick to the woman on his right, Joan Calvin's mother. "I remember wondering why Joany was late from school." She continued with a tale of worry and then terror as she learned what had happened, and her story was echoed in different versions of the same horror as the gourd passed from person to person, parent to parent.

Until it came to Bud Granger. He took the gourd gently from the man next to him, DaShawn Baker's father, and sat very still with it for a quite a while. Then, he said, "Pass" in a voice almost a whisper and moved the gourd to the next person.

As we moved around the circle, all of us who had not been there passed and all of the parents shared their memories from that day, the detail exquisite as a bejeweled egg because of how sharp the cut had been to their spirits.

The gourd's beads rattled as it shifted from hand to hand. I watched Charlotte watch the room. Her face was set with expectation. She knew—and so did I—that something mighty and gentle could wash over this room, if we let it.

Stu Tomlinson lay his hand over the hand of TJ Madison's mom when she passed the gourd to him, and she, for the first time, looked into his face. His words came slow at first, but as the burden of the years unfurled from his lips, they took on their own golden momentum. "I knew most of you back then. Or I knew the look of you, I guess I should say. Terra Linda wasn't that big. Still isn't."

A few of the parents' heads nodded.

"But I didn't know your children, and because of what I did, I never got to know them. Well, I knew you, Micah." He looked the man in the eye. "But not for good reason. I'm sorry for the part I had in what I did to your sister."

I felt a tiny crack give way in that room, a space for a little light to get in.

"We came up here that day because we were in the mind to make trouble. That's the truth of it. I was mad, but I didn't know why. I was just mad at everybody. It was cowardly to take it out on kids." He took a deep breath. "For that, I am sorry, too."

He nearly tossed the gourd to Javier next to him, and Javier held it a minute, honoring the words said before him, before passing it on to Darren.

I braced myself.

"I've been mad a long time." His voice was husky. "So long. And I'm no child." He looked at Tomlinson then, and a wave of something passed between them. I could almost see it move through the air.

"I'm trying not to be angry anymore, but our lives took a hard turn to ugly that day. No, not just that day. That whole time pushed us toward awful. It's hard to forgive all of that." He set his jaw. "But I'm trying."

On we went, with two more parents—Beatrice Norman's mother and father—sharing their memories of that day. Washing dishes. Coming home to see the police cruiser in the driveway. The fear. The confirmation of the worst thing.

I listened carefully to each person's words, tried to hold the space around my heart open for anything people shared, but I could feel myself leaning on around the circle. Waiting.

Finally, the gourd passed to Nicole, who shook her head and moved it into Merle Popson's hands. He didn't look up. He didn't move at all, just sat there with his elbows on his knees and the top of his head showing to the circle. His hair was mostly gone there in the middle, and I couldn't help thinking how sometimes we don't know the emptiness people hide where we can't see it.

"We decided to come up here at lunch. The three of us did. We had cut out of school to get a beer, and we got talking. Like Bud said, we was just so mad. So angry." His hands shook slightly, and the gourd beads rasped. "We didn't come up here with a plan. I can say that in all honesty, but we did have evil in our hearts."

I looked to the ministers in the room.

"It was my idea. I had an old hose in the car from some landscaping work I'd done in the fall." He looked up then. I saw his eyes move to Roberta's face. "We didn't mean to kill them. We really didn't. But that don't matter, I know. They are still dead."

The room grew both heavier and brighter then, even though nothing changed about the light outside.

Popson handed the gourd over to Brenda Taliaferro's father, and the circle closed by passing from her to me to Mom and to Isaiah. None of us said a thing.

Isaiah held the gourd in his upturned hand and took a deep breath. "Now, our question is what we do with what has been shared here. How do we hold it together? Hold these words, these memories, these confessions? As we move around the circle this time, maybe we could share how we are feeling just now."

I don't know how it happened that we agreed to this way, but each person spoke one word as the gourd passed through their hands.

"Heartbroken."

"Angry."

"Rageful."

"Relieved."

"Sad."

"Scared."

"Confused."

On it went as we lay those feelings into that circle, as if there was a fabric stretched tight amongst us.

In elementary school gym class, we used to play a game. The teacher had a big piece of parachute material, and we'd toss beach balls into it and then ripple that material so they danced around. Our goal was to not let them fall off the edge. It took everyone's attention and focus.

When the circle closed again on our emotions, Isaiah said only two words. "What now?"

The silences around our answers here were longer, deeper, richer. Most people said, "I don't know." Some said, "I need time." Others didn't say anything at all.

When the gourd reached Merle Popson again, I found myself anxious, hopeful. It took me all the silence in which he sat for me to know I was hoping he'd say, "I'm sorry." But he didn't. He didn't say anything at all.

As the gourd passed to me, I felt myself lean forward, the urge to make all this okay was pushing against my throat. I think I was seeking what Mom calls "closure" when she talks about her clients. I even opened my mouth to say something, but then, I looked into the stricken faces of my friends' parents. I saw the lines of grief etched deep around Roberta's mouth. I stayed quiet.

The room was heavy with silence, but it was an absence of sound that carried a different feel than when I'd first come into that school. Then, it had been a muffling, a forceful silencing. Now, now it felt like the silence we all need when we walk with our eyes open into grief. It's not the silence of denial any longer, where things must be hidden. It's the silence of openness, the sound that comes when the wind hits the trees on the top of a winter mountain.

We closed the circle with that round. Isaiah thanked everyone for coming, and the room slowly emptied. Lucille gave Charlotte a long, tight hug before she walked, without looking back, out of the school.

Mom and I stayed to help Micah lock up, and as we walked down the steps, I saw Stephen in his car. He nodded, started the engine, and drove away. We hadn't needed the police after all.

23.

The next afternoon, Javier dropped me off at Shady Run. This time, he didn't offer to stay.

I sat down at Charlotte's feet, joining the circle of children before her. She was reading *Horton Hears a Who!* to the kids, and as she read, she pulled her fingers through my hair as my head rested on her knee.

After a few pages, she set the book face down and open across her lap. "There's a lot of truth out there now, Mary," she said quietly, "and a lot of work can be done with truth."
I let out a long exhale. "Is it enough, though?" I gazed at the twelve sweet faces watching me.

"It'll have to be." She began reading again. I could see the curve of a smile on her face when I looked up at her.

Henrietta climbed into my lap, her thin legs sprawled out across the floor in front of us. I wrapped my arms around her waist and squeezed. As I pulled her close, I felt my hands give way and reach my own body, and my head slipped back before I caught it.

I watched the other children slide away, the air stilling further with each heartbeat.

Charlotte's voice continued to read Dr. Seuss' classic for a moment more. "They've proved they are persons, no matter how small."

"Bye," I whispered into the empty school.

Acknowledgments

First, let me say thank you to my father-in-law Galen, whose encounter with a ghost of his own inspired this series and whose hometown of Buena Vista, Virginia, is the geographical inspiration for the town of Terra Linda.

I also want to thank the Book Champions, the most stellar launch team in the world. They have supported this book since before it was even an idea, and I'm so grateful for their support.

Great thanks, also, to all the stellar historians, genealogists, and historic preservationists who inspire me every day. I especially want to thank the African American Historical and Genealogical Society, Preservation Virginia, and the Central Virginia History Researchers.

I owe deep thanks to my family – Daddy, Adrienne, Mary Lou, Galen, and of course, Philip – who lived this story with me.

Finally, I thank you, the person who has picked up this book and given Mary, Charlotte, and all their friends a chance to live in the world.

Discussion Questions

If you would like to discuss this book with a class, book club, or youth group, I'd be giddy. Here are some questions to get you started. Plus, I love to come talk to groups, so be in touch through Andilit.com if you'd like to see if we can work it out to come hang with y'all and chat about Mary and her experiences.

1. What do you know about the education of African Americans in your neighborhood, town, or county? Were there Rosenwald Schools where you live?

2. Why do you think Charlotte and the children were murdered? What were the killers' motivations?

3. In your experience, are people of color given fair treatment by law enforcement officers? By educators? By other citizens?

4. Who was your favorite character in the book? Why did you like them?

5. What role does slavery play in 21st century American society?

Enjoy ALL the books in the *Steele Secrets* series.
Available everywhere books are sold.

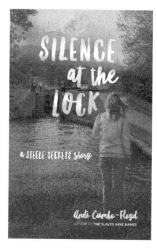

ABOUT THE AUTHOR

Andi Cumbo-Floyd is a writer, editor, and writing coach who lives at the edge of the Blue Ridge Mountains with her husband, 4 dogs, 4 cats, 6 goats, and 28 chickens. Her previous books include *The Slaves Have Names* and *Love Letters to Writers*. You can find out more about her books at andilit.com

63207180R00177

Made in the USA
Middletown, DE
25 August 2019